THE THIRTEENTH DAY

Aditya Iyengar is a writer who lives and works in Mumbai. To know more about him and his work, follow him on Twitter @adityaiyengar

THE THIRTEENTH DAY

A Story of the Kurukshetra War

ADITYA IYENGAR

RUPA

Published by
Rupa Publications India Pvt. Ltd 2015
7/16, Ansari Road, Daryaganj
New Delhi 110002

Sales Centres:

Allahabad Bengaluru Chennai
Hyderabad Jaipur Kathmandu
Kolkata Mumbai

This is a work of fiction. Names, characters, places and incidents are
either the product of the author's imagination or are used fictitiously and
any resemblance to any actual person, living or dead,
events or locales is entirely coincidental.

ISBN: 978-81-291-3475-2

First impression 2015

10 9 8 7 6 5 4 3 2 1

The moral right of the author has been asserted.

Printed by Thomson Press India Ltd., Faridabad

Contents

A Note to the Reader

Astronomical calculations have placed the Kurukshetra War to be around the year 3102 BC. Other sources place it between 900 and 2500 BC. For the purposes of this story, I have taken the period to be around 1000 BC, when India had just entered the Iron Age and the ruling classes were vying to obtain this new and powerful metal that would give them an edge over their neighbouring kingdoms.

Now coming to my story.

The Thirteenth Day is a retelling of the life of Abhimanyu within the story of the Kurukshetra War. As a media professional who's spent years creating different stories for brands and people, I had wanted to explore the process of fact becoming myth and wrote this as an analogy to modern times where we're constantly trying to engineer an 'image' of ourselves for a larger public. Mass media and now social media are the new instruments of the bards of our times, and in fact, on social media, we have become our own bards; weaving impossibly perfect narratives of our lives in this Selfie Yuga. Like the characters in the subsequent pages, we are forever conscious of the kind of impression we create for the public at large. Just take a look at any social media timeline. People cherry-pick pictures, articles and various quotes to depict how they feel about things. We want to be seen as successful professionals, dreamers, visionaries, travellers and do-gooders.

We are forever engaged in the creation of our own myth, in the telling of our own story, whether it's on a social networking website, or national television.

Myths are not fantasy. They are our day-to-day lives.

In this context, I felt that it would be interesting to explore the possibility of the Mahabharata as history rather than mythology. There was, or must have been, an actual war thousands of years ago that got repeatedly embellished in its retelling to become the story we know today. Over the years, men acquired supernatural powers and events became contorted to acquire new significance. Real weapons got replaced by astras with nuclear potential. Real people became rakshasas or celestial beings, Suyodhana became Duryodhana, and what was probably a small battle became a war that nearly wiped out every man in Bharatvarsha.

Perhaps that's what our ancestors had in mind when they narrated the Mahabharata. Maybe they too wanted to tell their own stories in grand terms?

They were human after all. Just like us.

I find it particularly apt in today's context, since we're desperately trying to find scientific explanations for flying vimanas and potential nuclear weapons. It seems we would rather have a past filled with great scientists than just great artists and writers who could dream up these wonderful and awe-inspiring creations. It's a strange irony: we're spending our time trying to find the truth in our past, but creating myths of ourselves in the present.

The events and characters of this novel are mostly faithful to the original story from the Mahabharata. Some minor characters and details of war are fictional. On the whole I've tried to capture the spirit of the times, rather than document it rigorously.

A big thank you to my agent Urmila Dasgupta of Purple Folio. Thank you, Rupa Publications, for taking on this work, Amrita Mukerji and Kadambari Mishra for editing it with a fine hand, and Maithili Doshi Aphale for the cover design. As always, thank you Amma and Ashvin, for reading it and providing me with endless support and encouragement. This book is for you.

Prologue

The old warrior lay on a bed of arrows.

At least, that's what the bards would say. He groaned softly and tried to adjust his position, then winced as a thick whip of pain jolted through his body. He was a young boy again, being pinched awake by his tutor in the middle of class. He chuckled at the memory, greeting it like a long-lost friend. Memories of his childhood had been scarce for some time now, and it was strange that this one had slipped through the usually impenetrable wall of his thoughts.

Truth is, Arjuna had panicked and fired more arrows than were strictly necessary. They were bronze tipped, not surprising considering iron arrows were in short supply in the Pandava camp. Arrow after arrow had rent through the iron breastplate, a couple had cracked open his helmet and lacerated his skull. He remembered swivelling around and then falling onto the black-red soil.

And then nothing.

His eyes had opened later, without his knowledge or consent. A number of concerned faces peered down at him. He tried to stand up but found that he couldn't. After a short struggle he realized that the the arrows that had struck him in the back were propping him up unevenly. He remembered picturing a cockroach writhing on its back waiting to be killed, and thinking it was funny and wholly inappropriate for a Kuru patriarch to feel this way. He tried to stand once again, but the arrows twisted within him and dragged him out of consciousness.

'Arjuna's masterpiece,' he thought to himself and chuckled. In the four hours since he had fallen on the arrow shafts, he had become a minor attraction at the battlefield. His body, along with the protruding arrows, had been heaved delicately by an entire platoon of soldiers to a tent that had been hastily set up on a small hillock overlooking the battlefield of Kurukshetra.

All the important kings of Bharatvarsha came and paid their respects to him—some out of reverence, most out of sheer curiosity. He had become a living, breathing installation; a morbid work of art. Ironic for one who had spent his life behind the stage rather than on it.

The battle had been suspended on that day given his unique status as grandfather to both sides of the battlefield and his eminence as a senior statesman of the Kuru empire. Medics from both camps had attended to him and had dislodged nearly all the arrows by now, squabbling every minute of the way on the line of treatment to be prescribed.

The arrows were gone, but pain still racked his body, thundering through him whenever he got too comfortable. He wondered how the bards were going to describe the horror and glory of Bhishma. Would they depict him stretched on a bed of arrows in elaborate paeans? Would they describe the pain that inhabited him and resurfaced without warning, as if playing a macabre game of hide-and-seek, thumbing its nose at him and running away? Would he be seen as a casualty of destiny, or its willing servant? Or, if they were generous, would he be seen as the man who did everything in his power to prevent the Kuru kingdom from its tragic inevitable end?

Strangely enough, he felt comfortable now, in a way he never had before. The weight that had straddled his shoulders for the past two generations had been lifted almost instantly as the first arrows scuttled his armour. Now he, Bhishma the Wise, the Magnificent, the Terrible, Conqueror of Kingdoms, Destroyer of Heroes, was helpless. The outcome of the Kurukshetra war fought between the Pandavas and the Kauravas was out of his hands.

Finally.

For ten days now, both sides had battled on the field of Kurukshetra, an even plain surrounded by small hills, agreed upon in advance by both warring parties for its proximity to the allied kingdoms and its relative distance from human settlements. Bhishma had insisted that the battle for Bharatvarsha should not affect the lives of its people. There would be no raiding or marauding. No great manoeuvring or outmanoeuvring. It would remain a private affair of the participating kingdoms and that was all. Battle would begin in the morning and end only as the evening approached.

The sound of footsteps interrupted his reverie. A figure opened the tent flap from the outside and sidled in. It took a few steps towards the bed, hesitatingly, like a child at a yajna, and stood mutely.

'If you're looking for a fight, you've caught me one day too late, putra,' Bhishma opened the conversation. He was in a chatty mood, expansive in his plight.

'I still wouldn't take you on, Grandsire.'

Bhishma recognized the voice. It was smooth as it was rustic; a singer's voice, but a country bumpkin's tongue.

Bhishma had never really liked Radheya, the king of Anga—Suyodhana's pet bully. An obnoxious little man who took pleasure in being insolent to the elders of the Kuru empire. Suyodhana himself couldn't rein him in. A few days before the battle, Bhishma had had an argument with him over troop placements and Radheya refused to take the field after that for the past ten days, a decision that was costing the Kaurava army dearly. Immature brat. Not even forty years back, one could have been executed for even stepping outside the camp to take a piss.

The old soldier took a deep breath and sighed, 'You're very kind, though my present condition suggests otherwise. What can I do for you?'

'I...I just came to see how you were doing, Grandsire.'

'I see...and how does it look like I'm doing, putra?'

Radheya grinned and shook his head wolfishly, 'Point taken sir...though, I think you took a few more in your back today.'

The one thing Bhishma hadn't missed was his idiotic sense of humour. Radheya no doubt thought he was being witty and sophisticated, but sarcasm wasn't Bhishma's forte and it seemed a wasted effort to counter wits without an audience in the vicinity. Besides, what use was all the anger now when nothing was in his control? Bhishma's face broke into a tired grin and wrinkles eddied across his face.

'Pah! Impudent boy. If I could just stand, I'd tan your hide.'

Radheya smiled. 'The reason I've come is I wish to put the past behind us. I'm sorry we clashed about troop placements. I have decided to take the field. I just wanted to let you know.'

'Decided to take the field? That's very considerate of you now. We could have done with your help ten days ago.'

'I'm sorry, but it wasn't all my fault. You didn't have to be so stubborn.'

Bhishma calmed himself. Now was not the time to lose his temper.

Not when he had a plan.

He sighed, 'I'm too old to bear any grudges, putra. And I reckon you're too young. But let's not talk about the battle for a moment—I suppose you know how you are related to the Pandavas by now, Radheya?'

'Yes, grandsire. I'm Kunti's, I mean, Lady Kunti's first child. But she abandoned me to avoid facing the wrath of her parents after an...ah, affair. She told me the whole story a few days before the war.'

'I see. Well, it's heartening to know that Kunti has finally decided to act like an adult. I didn't learn of your birth until much later. And when I did, it was from your Uncle Vidura who kept the fact a secret from everyone to protect Kunti's marriage to Pandu. My apologies for not informing you then. It hardly seemed necessary once Suyodhana brought you out from the stables and made you king of Anga. But none of that is important now. Think of the future, putra. You are related by blood to the five most powerful princes of Bharatvarsha who would welcome you with open arms and a kingdom. Doesn't it make you feel any differently about them? After all, they are your brothers.'

'The "brothers" you speak of want me dead.'

A long silence greeted this remark. Bhishma's face sagged

into deep thought and emerged after a little while with a wry smile.

'You know, Radheya, I've always kept an eye on you from that day, many summers ago, when you set foot in the archer's tournament. Not so much for your benefit, but my own.'

'Sire?'

'I'm proud of you, boy. I've seen you grow from a charioteer to king. And with none of the support the other children had. It's done me good to see Kunti's eldest triumph over all the misfortune life has thrown at him, to know that our stock is still capable of producing prodigies who can conquer the world with nothing serving them but the blood and blessings of their ancestors. But be realistic, putra. There is no chance of us winning now. The Pandava chariots are cutting up our forces like...'

'Like a scythe in harvest? I know, Grandsire, I've heard the slop coming from amateur poets in Indraprastha from my agents too. That's why I'm here. To make sure it doesn't happen... anymore.'

'By doing what? Adding to the tally of those lying in the mud at Kurukshetra? Listen to me, boy, spare everyone the bloodshed. Join the Pandavas, your real brothers, with your troops. They'll be more than happy to have you by their side. Then parley with Suyodhana and talk some sense into him. With a substantially weakened army, shorn of his best generals, dead as most of them are anyway, he will relent.'

He took a deep breath and continued, 'The Pandavas and Kauravas are fighting for a kingdom that isn't even theirs. You're the eldest son of the Kuru clan. The kingdom is your birthright. Take it and end this nonsense war.'

Millions of little campfires lit the killing grounds of Kurukshetra, forming a crude reflection of the stars in the night sky. Radheya took in this panorama and let the idea of becoming king sink in.

The war had really begun two generations ago when Pandu, the king of the Kurus had died leaving his brother, the blind Dhritrashtra the ruler of the kingdom. As Dhritrashtra grew older, the issue of succession became a matter of concern. Pandu had five sons, the Pandavas—Yudhishthira, Bhima, Arjuna, Nakula and Sahadeva. Dhritrashtra, however, had many more. Yudhishthira, as the eldest son of Pandu, had a strong claim to the throne. But Dhritrashtra's eldest son Suyodhana had a claim that could be taken no less seriously. The Kurus divided into two factions. The sons of Pandu called themselves the Pandavas to underline their claim to the throne as the sons of the original king of the Kurus; and Dhritrashtra's sons under Suyodhana called themselves the Kauravas to emphasize their status as sons of the Kuru dynasty and its proud lineage.

Over many bitter years, the brothers clashed. The kingdom was even sundered into two to preserve the peace. The western part of the Kuru lands, known as Kuru Jangala, was to be ruled by the Pandavas with the capital at Indraprastha; while the eastern part belonged to the Kauravas with their capital at Hastinapura. Matters regarding the Kuru nation as a whole would be presided over by a council of elders. It was a tenuous agreement at best, but one that Bhishma had hoped would keep the peace for a few years. However, the arrangement failed, and Yudhishthira lost his entire kingdom to Suyodhana in a game of dice and got the Pandavas sent into exile. After thirteen years, they had returned for their kingdom. The senior members of the Kuru council of elders including Bhishma and Drona rejected their claim. Suyodhana had ruled the empire for thirteen years, and to take the Kuru Jangala kingdom away from him now would ruin the stability that all of them in the council had fought hard to create. Left with nothing, the Pandavas declared war.

Bhishma continued, 'Once he learns the truth, Yudhishthira won't deny you your birthright. He plays by the book.'

'And Suyodhana?'

'At this stage, putra, even he has a feeling that he's about to lose the war. Take it from me, Suyodhana will just be happy that Yudhishthira won't get to become king. He may whine and grumble about it for a while, but even he will not be able to deny you your right. And he will not protest much especially since this arrangement would keep both his honour and kingdom intact. It will just add to his bloated sense of self-worth that he delivered the Kuru kingdom to its rightful heir. Carve up the kingdom fairly, with the lands in the east in the hands of the Pandavas, and the lands in the west with Suyodhana. Install yourself as their sovereign. And you will have saved the entire Kuru clan.'

The Lord of Anga cast his eyes towards the ground. Bhishma continued in a softer voice, sensing his reluctance, 'I know what I'm asking of you, son. But this war will not end well for your friend. The thought of betraying him weighs your decision, but end this war in the next two days and he will live to rule his kingdom yet again.'

'You make it sound so easy. Let's pretend for a moment that I go along with this plan. You actually picture me wandering over to Yudhishthira's tent saying, "Hey, by the way little brother, I'm on your side now", then face Suyodhana on the battlefield, convince him not to tear my traitorous head off and get everyone together for a jolly family reunion.'

Bhishma glowered at Radheya and for a moment, the great Lord of Anga, conqueror of the Kamboja barbarians, the Kirata mountain fighters, the ferocious Kalingas and Andhras of the south, the Paundras, Utpalas, Vahlikas, Mekalas and many more, wished he had never been born in this infernally complicated family.

'Do not mock me, insolent fool. This is the only way I see the war having a favourable outcome for all parties concerned. No honour lost. No reputations besmirched. And most importantly, no more lives taken.'

'Then explain how I go across and talk to Yudhishthira? The sentries of the Pandava camp would cut me to petals if I tried going there at night. And you can't expect me to break out and approach them openly on the battlefield. They'll think it's a trap and kill me anyway. Sending a message to their mother... I mean...our mother, and asking her to speak on my behalf would look like I'm playing some dirty trick.'

Bhishma relaxed and felt the pain glow inside him like hot embers. It was all going according to plan.

'You're correct. As I see it, putra, there is only one way. Capture Yudhishthira in battle. Bring him back to camp. Then speak to him from a position of power. Tell him the whole story of your birth, claim the throne and send him straight back to his army with all his weapons as a gesture of faith. He will confirm the details with Kunti and welcome you with open arms. It's that simple. The day after that, defect before the battle begins, in full view of both armies. Ask Yudhishthira to parley with Suyodhana on the battlefield.'

Bhishma drew a breath and grimaced, but continued:

'Suyodhana will relent. Especially when he finds himself short of the Anga troops and the only general he can rely on to win this war for him. Also, don't worry about convincing our boys. I had already drawn up another plan with Suyodhana and Shakuni a few days earlier to capture Yudhishthira on the field. You'll hear about it in the council tonight with some luck. Put your weight behind it, and God willing, you will be king.'

Radheya nodded in agreement and sat down heavily next to Bhishma. 'I...I'll think about it, Grandsire.'

Bhishma's voice took on a soft, paternal tone.

'Call me Grandfather, putra. At least now, act like a Kuru prince.'

Bhishma extended his arm towards Radheya, beckoning him to take it, and all the wisdom it represented. Radheya squeezed his grandfather's hand. A little harder perhaps than he had intended to, with the desperate relief of a lost child reclaimed.

THE TENTH NIGHT

YUDHISHTHIRA

Bhima would have said the palms of my hands were criss-crossed with leaves of pink. The picturesque aftermath of a day spent holding the grooved handle of a sword too tightly. But that, I suppose, is the raw extent to which his rough-hewn poetics could have described my state of being when Grandsire fell.

I was there when it happened. Not slaughtering Kauravas by the cartload like my dear brothers, but engaging them in less emphatic numbers nonetheless. A fair distance away, not close enough to be in the thick of that particular fight, but near enough to see Arjuna's arrows penetrate him. It's a memory I'll carry to my pyre.

I see Shikhandi wedging her chariot in between Arjuna's and Grandsire's chariots. She mounts her first arrow onto the bow with deliberate slowness, provoking Grandsire to give her fight. Fighting her does not agree with Grandsire's personal code of conduct, his dharma. A true Kshatriya, he cannot raise his weapon to attack a woman, and he scrupulously tries to avoid the encounter. Grandsire turns. Shikhandi fires, taking off a chunk from Grandsire's shoulder plate. She isn't to be denied on this day. She fires two arrows quickly, but both fly wide. Then, from behind Shikhandi's chariot, Arjuna starts his barrage. In the time it takes Shikhandi to mount one arrow and fire it, Arjuna dispatches three with unerring accuracy.

He is a short man with a thin moustache lining his lip, and eyes too old for his face. He wears a spotless white armour and dhoti and looks completely unexceptional. Until he lifts a bow.

To watch Arjuna at war is like watching an artist at work. His face is a maze of lines as he picks up and strings his bow. His eyebrows contort as he yanks the bowstring and then ties it with a tenderness that almost seems comical in contrast to the raging tempest mired on his visage. He inspects the bow and makes minor adjustments that I cannot fathom. He mounts an arrow and the expression changes. The lines are buried under his skin now. The eyes are clear; his vision almost ethereal as he looks straight into the horizon and not directly at any one target. He picks up his first arrow, draws the bowstring to the absolute tip of his ear and then you can see it become apparent in his eyes—a frightening serenity, an awareness of everything around him from the neighing of a horse to the displacement of sand by a nearby foot soldier's boot. The bolt shoots out of Gandiva visible only as a blur, and his hand has already plucked the next arrow from his ready quiver. Arjuna's unique arrangement of quivers on his chariot floor allows him to pick up arrows with ease. His bow looses bolt after bolt with unfailing, undiminishing rapidity. Like a pumping heart? Like a woodpecker? Like a machine? Like nothing anyone will ever see on this earth. The bowstring buzzes. It wails. It mourns the death of its victim, hapless to stop his fingers from taking advantage of it thus.

Perhaps I exaggerate a little.

No more than the bards at Indraprastha.

Today, the normally becalming spectacle of his destruction horrifies me.

I see the arrows hitting Grandsire, breaking his bow and shattering his quiver almost in the same instant. Grandsire's quiver falls from his chariot. I look at Arjuna and swallow my urge to yell at him to stop, to put his bow down, and not hurt our grandfather. I grip my sword tightly so that my nails bite into the grooves of the hilt. I see Grandsire getting hit with arrows, a red spatter of carnage yawning slowly across his armour.

He doesn't raise his hands even once in defeat. He calmly bends down and picks up a sword lying on the floor of his chariot even as the arrows drill into his frame. He gets off the chariot, getting hit all the time, and walks slowly with the intent of taking on Arjuna with his sword. With a lesser warrior, such an effort would have seemed pathetic. With Grandsire, it was magnificent. The arrows break his sword and his only chance at self-defence. An arrow dislodges Grandsire's helmet, gashing his skull. And from then on, arrows just etch themselves on his body. Grandsire doesn't struggle. He just stretches his arms out accepting them as an inevitability of fate. Almost telepathically, Arjuna complies. There is no malice. No vengeance. Arjuna pours his arrows into Grandsire, battering every inch of his banyan-like bulk. The warriors around Grandsire and Arjuna are transfixed by what is happening before them. Already planning the stories they will tell their disbelieving comrades. History… no…a legend is unravelling before them. The sheer awe of the spectacle stops everyone from their bloody task. Sushasana with his mouth open like a child watching a magic trick, Suyodhana's eyes shining with tears, helpless, Satyaki trying to catch a glimpse of Arjuna's fingers blurring with the bowstring. I see Grandsire catching Arjuna's attention with the merest of smiles. Arjuna acknowledges it, bowing his head ever so slightly. I see their eyes meet and not let go until Grandsire falls to the ground encumbered by the weight of his death.

And then the battlefield comes alive once again. I hear Suyodhana bawling for a medic and Sushasana with Guru Drona followed by a platoon of Kaurava chariots scrambling desperately to Grandsire's side even as Bhima and Satyaki make to intercept them. My own reverie is broken at this instant when my charioteer asks me if I want to join the fray. As if in a dream I whisper some instructions to him, words I'll never remember, but my chariot lumbers in the general direction of the fight.

I don't remember much of the fight after that but it couldn't have been very long. A parley was called and we spent the remainder of the day paying our respects to Grandsire.

I returned to camp after that and walked straight to my tent, a crude structure fashioned out of animal hide and wooden poles. A large bed with silk sheets and cotton pillows facing the entrance was its primary inhabitant. A tiger-skin rug made up the centrepiece and was strategically placed at the foot of my bed to intimidate visitors or at least suitably awe them. A writing table and stool were placed on the left side of my bed and my armoury—an unwieldy rack of wood—to the right. Tonight, my writing table was cluttered with missives. Unusual, considering I normally received just one letter a day, a combined effort from Draupadi, our wife, and Kunti, our mother. I, and each of my four brothers were required to put our thumbprints on this 'letter' we each received individually every night and send it back the same night through a messenger—a sign that things were well.

I sifted through the debris of palm leaves and parchments and opened one of them. It was a long-winded piece of fluff that said something about 'lending our assistance to your worthy cause. Hope you give us the opportunity'. The others read similar platitudes.

So, the lion falls, and the jackals swoop in. Bharatvarsha was in shock. The loss of Grandsire had given new legitimacy to our cause. Now that the war was tilting in our favour, the lesser kings of Bharatvarsha, the ones who were too timid to join us because of the might of the Kuru alliance, were ready to join hands with us.

I resisted the urge to dash off a response to my charming friends. A harshly worded message could have made new enemies for us. It was beneath my dignity to let these cowards, skulking in their palaces, grace the battlefield when all the hard fighting had been done by us. It was our fight. We would win this war alone, without any of their last-minute heroics.

My retainer Vishaka entered the tent and began to help me with my breastplate, silently unclasping the hooks around my back and shoulder. I removed my helmet and placed it on the bed. The cool air felt alien on my humid scalp.

In a weak attempt to lift my spirits, he tried making conversation, 'I've heard Lord Bhishma fell today, sire. May I offer my congratulations?'

'Congratulations? That's my grandfather who was nearly killed today. On my orders. By my little brother's hand. What exactly are you congratulating me for?'

'I'm sorry, my Lord.'

I calmed down. Vishaka had been subject to far too many of my mood swings. On his part, he avoided provocation as much as humanly possible, did his chores diligently, kept my armour buffed and was handy with a massage too.

'It's all right, I didn't want any of this...least of all to see my grandfather on the other side of the battlefield.'

He didn't understand this.

Victory for him was a good thing that overcame defeat. Much like good and evil. Loss of life was but collateral on the field of battle for the greater prize, glory. But he didn't say anything and simply nodded.

I removed my white linen tunic that stank of sweat and was dotted with tiny blotches of blood that looked like spots of kumkum. Vishaka prepared a poultice of haldi to clean my wounds. I had survived the day practically untouched. A spear had grazed my left arm and a couple of arrows had taken the great effort of piercing my iron breastplate to prick my skin ever so slightly. He began work and finished almost immediately. Pleased, I imagine, more for the speedy completion of the task and his potential return to idleness than his master's unblemished vitality.

I wanted to take in the mood of the camp, so I dismissed Vishaka, picked up a sheepskin shawl and walked out.

The camp was a creature that only came alive at night. Much like the parijat flower that blooms only after sunset. It spanned ten yojanas from end to end with borders, demarcations and fortifications. Like a small township sufficient in itself with rows of tents in different colours each representing our various allies. If you looked down from the skies it would resemble a pretty, multi-coloured flower. In the centre, lay our Indraprastha contingent, the tents a regal deep blue. The camp lay deserted during the day with a gaggle of followers and retainers cleaning up behind their masters. If their masters didn't return, the followers just packed up their master's tents and went back home, or alternately sought employment with another Kshatriya. Many a time, it was suspected that they looted the personal effects of their dead masters and sold it off to other buyers.

I walked directionless, seeking a familiar face. I could hear the sound of raucous laughter tearing through the invisible fog of calm that every camp unwittingly but painstakingly creates on the night before battle. Apparently some of the men had forgotten that their friends had died today, choosing instead to focus on the day's single positive outcome. Grandsire had instilled a rare kind of fear in our men. He was fairly good in his time no doubt; having defeated some of the fairly illustrious names of his youth, but was well past his prime now. It was no secret that Arjuna was a better archer. And so was Radheya. Drona was better if not at par, as were Ashwatthama, Satyaki and a number of other bucks making their future reputations. In the early days of the war, even young Abhimanyu had managed to make short work of him in a duel.

Among the people of Bharatvarsha, however, his reputation had assumed epic proportions, propelling him into the realm of legend. He couldn't lift an arrow out of a quiver without some minstrel going into raptures about the unfortunate consequences of the act. Grandsire encouraged these little odes to his greatness and occasionally even asked poets and songwriters to compose verses to his victories, and to go about the land singing them in high notes of hyperbole. With every new telling, his enemies started to become more and more supernatural and his victories became magnified to the stature of miracles. This was his most subtle act of brilliance. Grandsire knew that battles were as often won off the field as on it. And he also knew that a fearsome reputation, coupled with a stern countenance, could intimidate any foe.

His renown grew to the point that kingdoms would accept defeat without even taking to the field, relieved at the thought of not facing Grandsire, the harvester of death, the Terrible One who could (I once heard) 'shoot flame arrows from his eyes and fart tornadoes'. The thought amused me then, as it did in the dusty bylanes of our camp. An army of grown men quaking in their boots fearing a sexagenarian white beard who would have rather dandled an infant on his knee and played elephant to a tot's mahout than lift a bow and arrow. Personally, I don't think Grandsire cared too much for this reputation, though he went to great lengths to maintain it. For anyone born of this yuga, he would forever be the Terrible One.

Large spits of meat roasted in the open with enormous coal beds crackling in the sand beneath them. The spit turners sweated profusely, their muscled shoulders swinging rhythmically in the dust and night wind. The meat lumbered slowly around the spit while attendants massaged it with herbs and spices. A group of young soldiers sitting near a spit got on their feet and began chanting—Bhi-ma, Bhi-ma, Bhima, Bhima!

As was expected with men whom nature chose to endow with the bounties of spectacular physical health, Bhima was fairly conspicuous. He strode into their midst swinging his arms with the wild abandon that only the truly carefree rejoice in. A square, solid face tanned deep brown, riven by a thick black moustache that stood defiantly between his fleshy cheeks. Short, thick hair, pared almost to the scalp and big, liquidy brown eyes that bared his every emotion shamelessly, even when he wanted them to remain hidden. The eyes, however, were the last thing one noticed about Bhima.

Nearly the height of an elephant's shoulder, Bhima towered over every human warrior on the battlefield. His upper body was wide like the trunk of a tree, sprung with black hair, but tapered almost anti-climactically into a slender waist. This odd, almost comic, triangular physique was a great source of pride to Bhima who attributed it to heavy physical exercise and a rigid diet which he enthusiastically recommended to his brothers; and forced upon at least one nephew till he was told to keep his notions of physical fitness to himself.

His anomalous girth had earned him many nicknames. The one that stuck was Vrikodara, wolf belly, since it is said that the bellies of wolves are always lean, no matter how much they eat. Affectionate stories had spread about Bhima maintaining this lithe dancer-like waist by restricting his appetite at every meal so as to leave some food for the rest of mankind.

I had heard from at least four different sources that he could lift a fully grown horse several feet above the ground and crush it in his embrace—a feat I had never seen him perform. His mastery over wrestling was already well documented across Bharatvarsha and he was unarguably one of the finest exponents of gada-yuddha—mace warfare.

Tonight, he celebrated with the troops. Not because he felt no love towards Grandsire, but because, if I knew my brother, it would serve to boost morale in the camp. Bhima was always more of team player that way. More than Arjuna, and more than Nakula and Sahadeva who kept conspiring between themselves.

He lumbered up to the nearest barrel of Sura wine, lifted it up coolly and quaffed it to the delighted roars of our hero-worshipping lads. A thicket of hands sprung up around him, offering him meat and mugs, and the clamour continued, rousing nearby soldiers from their slumber. Our biggest threat on the battlefield was dead (in a matter of speaking). If they didn't celebrate this, God only knows what they would celebrate in the days to come, if they lived at all.

I walked up to him and ruined the moment for the soldiers. I was a curious figure in this camp. Most of the boys saw me as a statesman whom adversity had turned into a warrior. Most of the time, I was on the receiving end of a lot of sorry glances, which I soon learned to ignore. A couple of the boys even tried to help me on my chariot on the first day till a withering look sent them scampering.

After ten days of battle, the soldiers still didn't take me seriously as a fighting man. Most treated me with an exaggerated formality stemming from pity.

I hated it.

And at times, I felt envious of Bhima, who could be both a leader and also 'one of the boys'.

Vishaka once told me that there was a saying in our camp that Arjuna was the strategist, Dhristadyumna the organizer, but Bhima was the morale. The older soldiers had taken it upon themselves to explain this unique trinity to the newer ones in a less complex manner: if the army was likened to a human body then Arjuna was the brain, Dhristadyumna the belly, and Bhima ('*our Bhima*') was the very heart, because Bhima wept for all those who died under his command. He bled for the living too, putting himself directly in harm's way to ensure the safety of the boys in his charge. The soldiers in the army looked at him with great reverence, so much so that it had become customary for every soldier to glance at him and his lion battle standard for good luck before the day's battle started. When I asked Vishaka what part of the human anatomy the soldiers had ascribed to me in this fine metaphor, he told me that soldiers could be a crude lot and that some things are better left unsaid.

I placed my hand on Bhima's shoulder. He tore his mouth off from the barrel and looked excitedly at me, 'Ha! The war is ours now. This calls for a couplet, eh brother? What say?'

He cleared his throat and began loudly:

'There once was an old grandsire
Who protected some Kaurava liars
With Grandsire gone
How will they go on?
And who'll save them from my ire?'

The applause probably woke the sentries at the Kaurava camp. Drunk with success, and God knows how much wine, Bhima cleared his throat again, 'Wait, another one! Another one!'

Bhima fancied himself a poet, composing little ditties and couplets to mark the day's kills. A macabre misuse of intellect, but I wasn't going to stifle his indulgences.

Dhristadyumna came to my rescue. His aquiline features, the pride of the house of Panchala, creased with worry. The exertions of the past ten days had cut lines into his forehead and cheeks that normally came at a more advanced age. A thick red scar ran down his eyebrow across his face to his jaw, the work of a Naga battleaxe heaved at him in the course of battle.

He smiled shyly at us and said in his soft, whispery voice, 'Midnight council...my, er, my tent.'

Not a man of many words, my brother-in-law.

RADHEYA

I walked into our camp early on the tenth night. Grandsire's words making spider webs in my head. The only good thing to come out of the old stick's defeat and near death was that the day's battle had ended early, giving the troops more time to rest and get over the shock. The camp was silent tonight. You could probably hear a moth fart.

Our camp was situated beyond the eastern edge of the Kurukshetra plain, occupying several yojanas. The sons of Pandu had taken up the western side. They had a better location, I felt, fed as they were by constant supplies on the Yamuna. The winds also moved in our direction, so the stench of carnage invariably bottled up in our camp. Hardly deciding factors in the current scenario, since our supply lines were still holding strong, and that is what really mattered, but there was no telling how long this war would go on. I borrowed a courier boy's horse and rode hard towards the council tent in the centre of the camp. If I knew this army, they would have begun searching for culprits to blame before Grandsire's body had even hit the ground.

We had started the war with eleven akshauhinis. The ancient texts prescribed that ideally each akshauhini was to maintain 21,870 chariots, 21,870 elephants and 65,610 cavalry supported by 109,350 infantry—a total of 218,700 soldiers divided into ten brigades of 21,870 each called ankinis. The brainchild of, no doubt, some arse of a nobleman wanting to make life difficult for the quartermaster.

While we tried hard to maintain at least 100,000 men in each akshauhini, both our army and that of the Pandavas was closer to around 80,000 divided into eight ankinis of 10,000 each. As men died and kings deserted us, it became harder to stay true to even these numbers.

Then there were Atirathis and Maharathis. Members of the nobility who were good at killing people (as all good nobles should be) were called Atirathis. The title gave them a personal guard of up to 10,000 men funded by their respective kingdoms, and a reputation for murder they had to live up to every time on the battlefield. Members of the nobility who were so good at killing people that the bards and poets made it look like a fine art were given the title Maharathi. They got a personal guard of 60,000 troops and were targetted by every man on the opposing side.

Some of the richer members of the 'class' would just buy their titles or have it gifted to them. I had heard that they were even calling Yudhishthira a Maharathi in some parts. Useless coward couldn't hold a bow to save his life.

Both sides had a good number of Atirathis. We counted hundreds at the start of the war, including Bhagadatta, Kritavarma and Jayadratha. The Pandavas, too, were well-endowed with them—Ghatotkacha, Satyaki and even the woman Shikhandi.

Maharathis were fewer. I did a quick tally on my fingers. The Pandavas had only Arjuna, Bhima, Dhristadyumna, Drupada and old Virata; while we had begun with Grandsire, Drona, Shalya, Suyodhana and myself. Extravagant bounties had come up on all our heads but only one Maharathi had fallen in ten days—Bhishma.

Bhishma's presence itself was worth an akshauhini, though I'd never admit it to his face. The old man and I never hit it off, sparring against each other at every given opportunity. He never stopped questioning the nature of my support for

Suyodhana and I gave it straight back by taunting him about his spinelessness around the Pandavas.

Still, the old bugger was right. The only way to return home was by ending this war immediately.

And I owed Suyodhana that much.

It all began with a public archery tournament. I had entered the competition hoping to win a quick purse of money when the Kuru princes arrived to compete with much fanfare.

Most of them were average, even below par. The oaf, Bhima, took a muhurat to fire a shot and Sushasana didn't even know which end of the bow was up. But the crowd loved them. One of these boys would be their king one day.

The only brother who knew why he was there was Arjuna.

We met in the final round.

To defeat Arjuna in an archery tournament would have been humiliating for the Kurus. A few questions and some open purse strings gave them everything they needed to know about me.

And so, as I was taking my first shot at the target, Bhima stepped out of the audience and spoke, 'Hey suta...charioteer boy, stop horsing around.'

I turned and looked.

'This is a serious contest between Kshatriyas. There's no room for you here. Pack up and go before we make you leave.'

The words hurt. And I forgot that I had worked hard to get there and had more right to be at that tournament than he did. But I could do nothing. It was the command of a prince.

Just as I was getting ready to leave, a hand clasped my shoulder and held me back.

It was Suyodhana.

He looked at Bhima and said, 'He won't leave till he

completes the tournament. You need not concern yourself with Arjuna losing to someone out of the Kshatriya classes. Radheya is the new king of Anga.'

Back then, Anga was a small principality that didn't need more than a governer. Some people say that he made me king just to get back at Bhima. However, that matters little.

Suyodhana was the first person to see me as something more than what I appeared to be.

The council tent appeared in view. It was a large, square wooden house covered with cloth dyed in regal Hastinapura red that could accommodate the fifty-odd kings of our confederation. All surviving kings were required to report to the tent for our post-battle meetings. It was Grandsire's idea to preserve the myth that every king had a say in our cause when, in fact, he was the one who took all the decisions.

The numbers in the tent had been depleting steadily since the battle had started. Over the past ten nights, Grandsire had dominated these meetings. His age and experience meant that no king could dare to argue with him or press a point beyond reasonable limit. A fact he knew, and took advantage of. I had sat in as a silent spectator to these councils, more as Suyodhana's personal advisor than a council member. Tonight would be different.

The two sentries standing outside the tent grinned at me. They were my men, trained by my people and drafted secretly into Suyodhana's personal bodyguard to act as my eyes and ears looking out for the king. They had been the ones to inform me of Bhishma's fall almost as soon as it had happened. Their job also involved keeping me informed about troop movements in the Pandava corner and of the various happenings in the enemy camp through an intricate spy network they had made, the details of which they refused to divulge. I didn't bother with this trifle as long as the information was good and accurate, as it consistently had been over the past ten days. They had been serving Suyodhana for nearly four years now, but they had been in my employment for more than ten. I doubted that anyone knew about their relationship to me. No one in our army knew, certainly not the generals. I approached them. One was a short, thickset slab of a man with large side whiskers called Varahamira and the other was a tall reed who went by the name Shatrujeet.

'So,' I asked, 'is the circus gathered?'

Shatrujeet grinned, 'They've been at it for two hours now. Cheeping like parrots. Where have you been?'

Varahamira interrupted, 'Forgive him, my Lord, respect still does not grace the precincts of his tongue, nor wisdom, his thick stupid skull.' He glowered at Shatrujeet to emphasize his point. They were an odd couple, those two. Varahamira was polite to a fault, loyal as a puppy, knowing his place and sticking to it with a tenacity that would have done old Grandsire proud. Shatrujeet had a tongue that constantly tested my patience.

I waved off the remark. Varahamira started mournfully, 'My Lord, as my colleague pointed out, they have been discussing the consequences of today's events for over two hours now and have enquired about your whereabouts from time to time.'

This time Shatrujeet interrupted, 'It's a good thing the walls are so thin at places…allows us to listen in without being found out. If the army came to know what was being discussed there in the name of 'strategy', they would turn tail and scamper. Everyone's blaming everyone else. Started with a couple of princes telling Sushasana that he could have saved Grandsire by getting riddled with arrows in his place. Lord Suyodhana is standing up for his brother and so is Shalya, but the younger princes won't listen. Oh, and they're all looking for you now to see if you'll take the responsibility for Grandsire's plight since no one else is doing it.'

Varahamira nodded his head, 'Among the names discussed yours *has* featured prominently, sire…even though you weren't actually on the field of battle. They believe your refusal to take the field cost Grandsire. Apart from that, very little has happened. Guru Drona stepped in a little while ago, but we haven't heard anything from him. Complete panic is threatening to ensue.' Then lowering his eyes, he added gravely, 'It would be best if you entered now.'

I rubbed my palms and blew into them. It would be a long night.

The sabha was in full swing when I arrived, our allies having taken sides already. Nearly all of them were shouting at each other, cawing like monkeys in a menagerie. At the northern end of the room was a platform on which was installed a seat which, before tonight, had been occupied by Grandsire. Rows of hard wooden chairs were placed before it for our thirty-odd remaining allies. Couches, felt Grandsire, were not fit to warm a warrior's buttocks during war, leading our allies to grumble about soreness at the end of each night. A Speaking Staff was normally used to control the flow of conversation, but it wasn't doing much good tonight. In the centre of the platform, Suyodhana stood thumping the staff repeatedly on the carpet in an attempt to bring the meeting to order. Next to him, Guru Drona sat in padmasana on the floor with his eyes closed, muttering under his breath. Sushasana was sitting beside him with an expression that a dying calf may have taken pity on while Shalya rubbed his shoulder and spoke in his ear.

My arrival may have passed unnoticed as the herald announcing my entry gave up after a few feeble attempts at making his voice heard over the din. Not wanting to attract the attention of the warring confederates, I slunk across the room, keeping to the wall, bowing my head deep.

Chandravarma, a minor king who had contributed a few thousand chariots and his own limitless stupidity to the cause was trying to make a point, '...Prince Sushasana's carelessness in the protection of Grandsire has been noticed by all. The prince seeks glory, and a chance to do battle with Bhima, that is all. He does not have the maturity to do what is in the best interest of the army, and today, we have to bear the unfortunate consequences of his action.'

The noise grew even louder, many voices in agreement, a few in squashed dissent.

Suyodhana strode up to Chandravarma and hit him hard between his eyes with the staff.

The noise evaporated in an instant. Suyodhana loomed over our prone ally, waved the staff in front of his eyes, and said with quiet ferocity, 'This is the Speaking Staff. In this council, you do not speak unless you are given the staff.'

Suyodhana had a strange beauty to him. Even the Pandavas would admit to that. He had large eyes that could hold no sadness for long, a long straight nose and thick lips covered by a beard that framed his mouth without running over his cheeks. He was very careful about his looks, and I think that his skill with the mace came from wanting to avoid being hit on the face. I knew for a fact that his black armour with gold stripes and matching dhoti was specially created for him by an armourer in Mathura because Suyodhana wanted to die looking his best.

He glared at the other kings in the room, challenging them to contest him, which none of them did, petrified as they were of his rage. An uneasy silence filled the hall.

Then Guru Drona spoke in his patient rumble, 'Putra, this is a council of kings—the apex of civilization. You do not strike an ally down, no matter how unbecoming his conduct.' As one, all heads turned towards Guruji. 'Ah, I see the king of Anga has finally deemed us fit to be graced with his presence. Yes, you, Radheya, don't try and play chameleon.'

So the old fox was play-acting meditation, sensing the mood of the room before committing himself to an opinion. Cunning old bugger.

My move. 'Well, I could hardly interrupt the conversation when more important people like yourself chose to sit silently. Besides, as he just pointed out, Suyodhana did have the Speaking Staff.'

Suyodhana grinned and shook his head. Chandravarma was stirring in one corner, with a huddle of minor kings nursing him back to consciousness.

Guru Drona got up and took the staff from Suyodhana. He looked at me and smiled. A set of white teeth rolled out of his greying beard, 'This person, for one, is very keen to know what you have to contribute to this council. Or did you not know there was a war going on? It's been ten days of war you've successfully avoided till now. Skulking in your stables eh, suta? Ha! Old habits die hard.'

It was a poor attempt at humour; undoubtedly employed by Guruji to portray himself as a man who was making light of a very difficult situation. The sniggers that issued from the mouths of my allies—those near me were wise enough to restrain themselves—came more out of relief than any real appreciation of Guruji's comic talents.

I had heard suta remarks more times than I cared to remember. But my skin still hadn't thickened sufficiently to mask the flush on my cheeks.

I was born to Queen Kunti—the result of an affair with a nobleman. To conceal their little tryst, I was given away to be 'never-heard-from-again'. An old charioteer called Adhiratha adopted me and his wife named me after herself. So I became Radheya, son of Radha, and spent my childhood in the stables learning my father's trade. If life had gone on in that fashion, I would have been a suta, a charioteer like my father, married a nice girl and led a peaceful life.

I wouldn't be standing in this sabha feeling like a school boy before a thrashing.

Drona was practising archery in the forest that morning when I had gone to collect wood. He was younger back then. He wore a saffron dhoti and carried a bow in his hand. There was nothing extraordinary in it. A brown-coloured piece of animal bone and wood, wearing the dullness of a well-used instrument. He placed his toe on the base of the bow and curved the top end to meet the bowstring. When the string was tied, he pulled back the string and let it twang.

I can hear the sound even now.

He took out an arrow and fired it into a wooden bull's eye some few metres away. He did it slowly and I could see all the muscles in his arm flex and fade through the skin. Each arrow hit the centre of the bull's eye, at the same place. I watched, completely in awe of his performance. I don't think he even noticed me. After he finished practising, he walked away and probably forgot about it. But it left a lasting impression me. The thought that some day I could be like that—graceful yet deadly—stayed with me.

I let the remark pass along with the muted giggles of our allies. We had bigger concerns at hand. 'Guruji, I am here to serve the Kauravas. Now that Grandsire is not on the field, my enmity with him is at an end. I will bring my Anga contingent into battle and submit to the authority of my commander-in-chief.'

This created a stir in the hall. Suyodhana took the staff from Drona and banged it hard on the floor once again. 'Welcome back, Radheya. Better late than never.' The room began to murmur and Suyodhana banged the staff on the ground again and growled menacingly at the gathered kings, 'The purpose of this assembly is to appoint our new commander-in-chief. Would anyone wish to nominate themselves or any of our allies assembled here?'

The room grew silent for a few minutes. The younger kings wouldn't dare put themselves up for the reckoning, instead hoping for the patronage of some of the more ancient ones. In truth there were only a few names that could be considered seriously. I looked around scanning the faces. There was Suyodhana, but he would never nominate himself for the task, and his lack of tactical sense ensured that no one else would either. The rest of his brothers were not senior enough to vie for the position with the possible exception of Sushasana. Unfortunately, Sushasana had been given the responsibility of protecting Grandsire today, and had failed miserably at the task. He was lucky to be breathing in the tent tonight much less being given the command of the remaining akshauhinis of Bharatvarsha's finest.

There was Jayadratha, Suyodhana's brother-in-law, the king of Sindhu. He was a major contributor to our armed forces with his cavalry troops and horses, but was no match to Bhishma in stature. The fact that he had been humiliated in a melee with the Pandavas before the Kurukshetra war would also have worked against him. Then there was Kritavarma, the general of the Narayani Guard—the best troops in our confederacy.

There was Shalya, an uncle of the Pandava twins Nakula and Sahadeva, who found it more economically beneficial to join our army, and Shakuni of Gandhara, uncle of the Kuru princes, spewer of venom, instigator of hate, and after Suyodhana, my greatest ally in the ranks. While all of them could stake a claim to the top job, I knew of just three people who stood a serious chance based on seniority—Drona, Bhagadatta and I.

Drona, the acharya, head guru of the Kuru family. He was a Brahmin schoolteacher who had found his calling in destroying armies. For years, he ran the best military college in Bharatvarsha at Hastinapura under the patronage of the Kurus. Its reputation was so illustrious that even his enemies sent their children to humbly prostrate themselves in the dust before him and learn at his feet. There was no one better qualified to run the army than him. Even Bhishma had said so, many times, to which Guru Drona replied by stroking the nest beneath his chin and protesting strongly, invoking Grandsire's seniority and battle experience as contrary evidence. But behind that reluctance lay the simple knowledge that no man could unite this bickering mass of confederates better than Grandsire. Sketching out intricate battle plans and marshalling troops was just a part of the responsibility. Motivating the kings, most of whom had never been in anything more serious than cattle raids and border skirmishes, to come back every day and shed their blood for him; that was what made Grandsire the only man in Bharatvarsha fit to command its largest confederation of troops. But now, with the Terrible One gone, there really was no longer anyone better than Drona to take control of this army.

Unless one considered Bhagadatta.

The king of Pragjyotisha was the oldest man on the field of Kurukshetra and perhaps the only man to have unsheathed his sword as many times as Grandsire. Like Grandsire, the old king of Pragjyotisha was no senile dodderer. The Elephant King was what we called him. His akshauhini of elephant warriors had been used as shock troops in the initial days of the war and had caused much destruction among the Pandava front line. Varahamira told me that the elephants had evoked such fear in the Pandava camp that they had actually strung together a special division commanded by Bhima for the sole purpose of containing Bhagadatta's rampaging beasts. Not one to stay at the back directing troop traffic, Bhagadatta swaggered across the field on his silver-bedecked elephant, Supritika, seeking out duels with the most renowned fighters in the Pandava army. To his credit, he had defeated many of them including the half-wit commander they called Dhristadyumna.

I liked the old man. He was a cheery boozer with any number of stories from pre-history and not one content to rest in the vanity of his past. After Bhishma, he was the most experienced campaigner in our camp. Unfortunately, he also displayed a reluctance to accept the mantle of leadership, preferring instead to go out and derive savage glee from wrecking the Pandava army. 'They won't promote me out of a fight,' the bloodthirsty old tyrant had once told me. Of course, if too many kings insisted on his leadership, there would be little he could do, except take up the sceptre.

And then there was me, the man no one wanted to nominate for the role, but were grudgingly willing to accept if no one else was willing or able to take command. I had won over thirty battles and impressed my might upon five major kingdoms in Bharatvarsha. Arrow for arrow, I was the best chariot archer in the world, and the best independent commander of Chariot Corps. More significantly, I had defeated armies the size of the Pandava forces on a number of occasions in recent years, unlike Drona and Bhagadatta who had entered the battlefield rusty from the excesses of peaceful living. I knew how modern armies fought. I had fought in them, I had fought against them and that was an edge that neither Drona or the lord of Pragjyotisha could lay claim to. This was something all the allies knew, and more importantly, Suyodhana.

Finally, with characteristic impatience, Suyodhana declared, 'It is evident to me that there are only two kings who will be able to lead this army.'

YUDHISHTHIRA

We took our places inside the council tent. Twelve cushioned couches, a small luxury permitted in these strenuous times, were arranged in a circle a little distance from one another. An attendant glided across the room with a tray carrying cold pomegranate juice and honeyed barley cakes, presenting them to the kings assembled. I suppose the only advantage of having only a handful of allies was the fact that there were fewer heads involved in making decisions. I could only imagine the chaos in the Kaurava camp tonight without Grandsire.

Early on, while congregating our forces at Upaplavya, in our ally King Virata's kingdom of Matsya, we had decided to restrict the war council to include only twelve kings. While some of our minor allies grumbled about being left out of the decision-making body, the strength and overall experience of our war council allayed their concerns.

There was me and my brothers—Bhima, Arjuna, Nakula and Sahadeva. As the prime beneficiaries of the conflict, it was only natural that all five of us be included.

The other members of the war council were Drupada, the king of Panchala and our father-in-law, his eldest child, the lady Shikhandi, who managed the Panchala troops, and Dhristadyumna, Drupada's eldest after Shikhandi and the commander-in-chief of the entire army.

He was a curious one, my brother-in-law, a man of average height and build, soft-spoken and polite to a fault, regarding every question or comment placed at him with serious thought and a diffident smile, which, it seemed, took all the effort in the world to conjure. Yet, in matters of war, especially the theoretical and logistical aspects of it, he was exceedingly competent. At least that was what Arjuna thought, and in the minds of most, that was enough. It also helped that the numbers brought in by his father

Drupada accounted for most of our original seven akshauhinis.

Apart from the Panchalas, there was King Virata, the ruler of the Matsya kingdom, the next largest contributor to our cause. A quiet, brooding kind of man given to occasional fits of violent temper. At seventy-odd years of age, Virata had the distinction of being the oldest soldier in our army and, as the joke went, had probably been forgotten by Yama, the God of Death. He was still able to lead from the front, though, and willing to prove it to anyone who thought otherwise.

Satyaki represented the Yadava confederacy who supplied troops to both sides of the field. A good soldier, if slightly unhinged. I never saw him upset or nervous on the battlefield. He seemed to treat the war like it was a game, chatting with his victims as he made to kill them, occasionally even letting them go, to Dhristadyumna's annoyance.

Then there was Prince Chekitana of Chedi, the youngest of our council, he of the upper lip yet unwilling to yield hair. His father had committed to our cause on the condition that his son be given a place in the main council. The boy knew his place. He did not offer his point of view, and questioned strategy more as a student than as a stakeholder.

The twelfth and final member of our council was, in my mind, probably the most important—Krishna, a Yadava prince like Satyaki, and a cousin of ours. His cunning had saved thousands of men over the past ten days and resulted in the slaughter of over twice as many. But more importantly, his understanding of the frailty of the royal ego and ability to gently guide not one but many of them towards common ground made him invaluable. Whenever a council meeting threatened to disintegrate into chaos, it was it was to him that we'd look for clarity.

His slight but lithe figure and dark, almost blue complexion was a calming presence in our camp, lifting the morale of the troops ever so often. He was a fine warrior in his own right, a good bow and swordsman.

What really set him apart was his skill as a charioteer.

Krishna was like a god behind the reins. Twisting and turning his chariot through odd angles and narrow spaces, balancing it on one wheel and pirouetting, cutting through enemy ranks while avoiding their long spears and arrows. If Arjuna was the best archer on wheels it was because Krishna held the reins that gave them life.

Dhristadyumna began the meeting, 'As you all know by now, we've, er…we've made our first real breakthrough of the war today.'

Drupada piped in, 'Yes, well done, son; absolutely inspired leadership, putting young Shikhandi in front of Arjuna. Excellent planning.' He looked around hoping to see similar acclaim issue forth from other members in the tent, most of whom smiled indulgently. Dhristadyumna winced and followed it up by blushing a deep crimson. Drupada played the proud parent much to his son's deep, if often unexpressed, annoyance.

The plan had been Krishna's, who sat admiring his feet, not taking credit and letting Drupada roll on with the bombast. I don't think he actually cared. He just wanted the war over. He had noticed Bhishma's reluctance to confront Shikhandi over the past ten days and had suggested the plan of using Shikhandi as a barrier behind whom Arjuna could fire safely at Bhishma.

My father-in-law hadn't believed in it then. It was hard to argue with it now. Dhristadyumna, desperate for a plan, had actioned it.

He continued in his soft, cultured monotone, 'With Bhishma out, they will probably hand over command to either Guru Drona or Bhagadatta. If our sources are to be believed, Radheya may also make his first appearance on the field.'

It wasn't good news but the council seemed relaxed. For the past ten days we had fought in clenched expectation of his arrival. Now he was here, and the Kauravas had no cards left to play.

I looked at Arjuna and found everyone doing the same. Arjuna looked away uncomfortably. It was an unspoken agreement that Radheya, or Karna as he was more popularly known, would be his personal feud. Just as Suyodhana would be Bhima's. Radheya's ability with the bow had initially been compared to Grandsire's and Guru Drona's. The comparisons were now being made with Arjuna himself. A matter that Arjuna wanted to test, though he would never admit it.

Bhima scratched at his chin, 'We can finally kill them all. Day's turned out better than I thought. I'll tell Draupadi.'

Draupadi...dear, darling Draupadi...the reason why this war was being fought in the first place, at least in the words of the bards these days. Beautiful, long-suffering Draupadi marrying the five of us, on the insistence of my mother Kunti and her father Drupada to strengthen our alliance; sad, indomitable Draupadi, shamed in a throne room at Hastinapura with the beast Sushasana pawing at her sari; angry, confused Draupadi staring at me across the sabha hall. And then not looking into my eyes again.

The memory of it makes me cringe. Not long after setting up our kingdom in Indraprastha, we, and our cousin Krishna, had been invited to Hastinapura by the Kauravas. The day had begun without incident, until the gambling began. Maybe it was the wine but I found myself betting away everything I owned, from iron mines to elephant brigades and finally even Indraprastha. No one believes me but I honestly thought that the game and the stakes were not to be taken seriously. I thought it was a cruel exercise disguised, as so many of these are, as a harmless tease that we had to endure as guests of the Kauravas. If I refused to play, it would look as if the 'old stick in the mud' was throwing a tantrum again, so I had to keep piling my bets higher to show my enthusiasm.

After I had 'lost' my kingdom, we started betting for people. Again, I believed it was completely harmless. Arjuna tells me I should have drawn the line there. But I tell him that it would have looked as if I was taking the game seriously. No, I had to keep up the charade as long as they did.

Shakuni, my opponent, beat me every time. I gambled away my brothers and finally even Draupadi. At this point I expected the game to end with a few jokes at my expense. The next thing I knew, Draupadi was being dragged out from her seat by Sushasana.

We were stunned. Suyodhana and Radheya were jeering that I had just lost my kingdom and family and everyone in the sabha was witness to that. My brothers huddled around me as some of the senior members of the sabha shook their heads in agreement and others in disapproval. It all became surreal.

Sushasana began pulling off Draupadi's sari, claiming her as his slave, and I did not know how to react. Thankfully, Krishna intervened and pulled Draupadi out of Sushasana's reach even as Bhima howled and went after him. The sabha rose and broke the two of them apart.

We were issued a formal apology, but the senior members of the Kuru council, including Bhishma and Guru Drona, ruled that since I had acted irresponsibly and made a bet and lost my kingdom, I didn't deserve to rule it and sent me and my brothers into exile for thirteen years. It was all a ruse. We had been neatly manipulated and robbed of our kingdom to keep Grandsire's precious peace.

They've laughed at me ever since...for losing everything in a game of dice.

In the next thirteen years, I shook off my naiveté. And while Suyodhana spent his time expanding his empire through war, I expanded ours through my family of five. We married into the Matsya kingdom and the Yadava confederacy and promised trade privileges to the king of Chedi. When we returned, my family was a coalition of the largest kingdoms in the land.

RADHEYA

I hadn't really expected my name to be in the running when Suyodhana mentioned that there were two likely candidates for the post of commander-in-chief. Not least because I'd just returned to the army after a spell of insubordination. If anything, I was expecting to hear the names of Drona and Bhagadatta. So when he announced 'Drona' and 'Radheya', I was genuinely surprised. What surprised me more was the fact that there were no sarcastic comments in my direction from the allies. If anything, they appeared grateful in the fawning manner of the truly desperate.

Bhagadatta came up to me and cackled heartily, 'Well, boy, nine akshauhinis to your name now. Or is it seven? No matter. Excited?'

Before I could answer him, a set of loud thumps broke every thread of conversation passing through the room. Suyodhana wielded the Speaking Staff.

'Now, we choose. If anyone has any objections to the names put forth, or would like to add any more names now, please do so immediately.'

Murmurs filled the room. Grandsire hadn't needed a Speaking Staff to control his audience. And I could see Suyodhana was getting irritated playing traffic officer to our allies. He stood silent, arms on his hip, and glared out at the room as he did whenever circumstances did not agree with him. A tantrum hung in delicate balance. Drona sensed as much and intervened, 'Come, come. Let's have it out then. We need a leader before the next yuga. '

A couple of senior allies conferred with each other and raised their hands. Bhagadatta caught their eye and made a gesture ever so slightly with his fingers. The allies bowed their heads and stood silent after that.

After a brief pause, Drona continued, 'So, I assume that Suyodhana's choices are acceptable to everyone gathered here?'

I don't know whether he was genuinely trying to end the meeting or obliquely asking the council to reconsider, even deny me. In any case, the crowd rumbled their assent.

'Well then, let's make it simple. Let us have a show of hands to elect either Radheya or me as your commander.'

He had tricked me. I glanced casually at the gathered

assembly. Their faces were like stone. No one here would vote against him, not in front of him at least. Neither would they presume to ask for another means of selection. It was inevitable; a public vote wouldn't swing any way but his.

But I didn't want Drona to think that he had scored one over me.

'Before we start, I would like to say that I have been out of the war far too long. And, it wouldn't be right for me to take on command when veterans like Guruji are still around to lay waste to our enemies. I submit completely to Guruji's authority and am here to serve the army in whatever capacity he wishes.'

That said, I turned towards Guruji and bowed.

I don't know who was more surprised—Suyodhana, who thought that I was going to walk out of the council, never to return, if not given command, or Drona, who probably realized that he had not the slightest idea what game I was playing.

Suyodhana gaped at me disbelievingly, and then clapped his massive hands together. 'And so it shall be my friend, so it shall be! Allies of the house of Kuru, we have our commander!' The allies herded around congratulating Drona who looked at me with a puzzled expression, not knowing what to make of this new development.

Truth is, it would be a lot easier for me to go about capturing Yudhishthira without having to worry about deploying an entire army. Let Drona have his akshauhinis. I would have a kingdom. All that remained was getting everyone to decide on the plan.

Drona separated himself from the crowd and sat casually on Bhishma's seat on the platform.

He spoke briskly, as if he was addressing a bunch of brats from his gurukul, something that reassured our allies no end.

One even asked Drona whether they could bring their own couches in here tomorrow night, a comment which he ignored.

'Let's get down to business. We can't let the Pandavas think they've won already, can we? Suyodhana, you mentioned something earlier about a plan?'

Suyodhana nodded.

'Well, tell us already.'

Suyodhana gripped the Speaking Staff and addressed the sabha, 'Before Grandsire Bhishma's departure from the field, he had discussed a plan with me and Lord Shakuni of Gandhara. The plan can bring an end to the war in the next three days, if executed properly. It was still at a very raw stage of development when we had discussed it and the events of the day haven't given me a chance to really flesh it out. But now, since Grandsire's counsel is no longer with us, I feel the proper thing to do is to discuss this plan amongst ourselves and bring it to fruit. Grandsire had faith in this idea, and it would have been his desire to see us follow it through.'

Now it was our allies' turn to get surprised. Most of them probably didn't expect a plan to come up so soon. To have a strategy in place for tomorrow's battle, and that too sealed and approved with Grandsire's blessings seemed almost too good to be true.

Suyodhana continued, 'As you all know, the cause of the Pandavas rests with the sons of Pandu. Over the past ten days, great warriors like Guruji and Grandsire and the likes of me, the Lords Sushasana, Bhagadatta and Kritavarma, have tried, unsuccessfully, to rid their army of one of them. Arjuna and Bhima are the most difficult to kill, surrounded as they are by the Indraprastha Chariot Corps. Each of you knows how formidable they are individually too. Nakula and Sahadeva are mostly placed in the reserve and come out for hit-and-run manoeuvres with the cavalry. To predict their movements and pin them down, again, would involve a lot of resources.'

Our best chance of getting any one of the Pandavas therefore is Yudhishthira. He has proven quite comprehensively over the past ten days that he is the weakest link in their army. He has more troops around him than any of the other Pandavas, including two Panchala princes guarding his wheels at all times. He is normally placed near the centre of the army where the fighting is limited, where he can do no harm, and more importantly, where no harm comes to him. The plan that Grandsire Bhishma and myself were contemplating was to strike fast at Yudhishthira, during the thick of the battle, eliminate the people around him and take him prisoner.'

He let the words sink in, and before doubt crept in to undo their effect, he spoke again, 'When the Pandavas hear of their brother's capture, they will parley to exchange him. Which we will, for peace and the kingdom.'

The allies began to murmur.

'We have thought it through. Yudhishthira is next in line for the throne in their eyes. To capture him would be to defeat their cause entirely.'

The room went quiet.

Suyodhana's brother, Yuyutsu spoke, 'I think it will work.'

No one had really asked for his opinion. Yuyutsu was an insufferable twerp. Before the war began, he was the only one who spoke against it, whining against its unfairness to his cousins. Eventually, it had come to Suyodhana telling him that the war would happen with or without his approval, and he should decide once and for all, which side of the battlefield he wanted to stand on. Not surprisingly, he chose the side with eleven akshauhinis but still grumbled when given a chance. The other kings called him a Pandava behind his back.

The uncertainty that had clouded the room now seemed to drift away slowly. As Grandsire had predicted, all the kings had begun warming up to the possibility of winning this war without spending more troops. Their imaginations were whirring now. They could visualize the end of the war and that too with an almost artlessly simple stroke left to play. Yes, it was so easy.

Suyodhana turned to Drona who hadn't reacted and merely stroked his beard, as he tended to do when he was in deep thought. 'Guruji, we must allocate at least an akshauhini of troops entirely to the capture of Yudhishthira. The troops will comprise of cavalry and chariots to let us strike and return quickly. The Sindhu Cavalry from Jayadratha's contingent or Shakuni's Kamboja Raiders along with our own Kaurava Chariots are my recommendations for this regiment which, with your permission, I will personally command, Sushasana being my lieutenant.'

Drona didn't say anything. Lost in his reverie, he continued to pass his hand over his beard, curling its strands absent-mindedly. The whole room waited in silence for a few minutes. Finally, a rumble issued, 'I'm not quite convinced with this plan. Capturing the eldest brother of the Pandavas will prove more than a match for our troops. Your akshauhini will be obliterated before it even comes close to the Pandava centre. Men are precious these days. We've conscripted nearly every able man in Bharatvarsha, and we aren't going to get any more. I'm all for bringing this war to a close without shedding any more blood, but this is not the way to go about it.'

'If Grandsire believed in it, I think we can too, safely.' All eyes turned towards me. 'Capturing Yudhishthira is far easier than killing five Pandavas, which we will have to, if the plan is unsuccessful, in any case. We have a real chance of ending the war within the next few days.'

The kings who had been deflated after Guruji's lack of enthusiasm for the idea suddenly became animated. Shakuni, king of Gandhara and uncle to the Kauravas, rose. 'It is the only way, Guruji. Unleash my raiders upon the rabble that Yudhishthira calls an army, and he won't stand a chance.' The other kings took up his call and stood up as well, loudly exclaiming in favour of the plan.

Drona took a deep breath, 'Very well. If this is what everyone wants, then I shall not stand in the way. But I cannot lead an army into a plan I don't believe in. So I ask you to elect another commander. Preferably one who approves of this foolhardy enterprise.' Having said this, he turned his head in my direction.

Cunning old fox. His experience was crucial and he knew it. We would have had to change the plan, but for the timely intervention of Suyodhana's temper that had been bubbling discontentedly for a while now.

'So you're leaving us now, Guruji? First Radheya doesn't take to the field for ten days, and now it's your turn? I'm tired of people coming and going from this army at their pleasure as if it were a bloody playground.'

'I didn't mean it that way, putra, all I said was...'

'Don't tell me anything! Are you with us or not, Guruji? That's all I want to hear.'

The fox was cornered. Suyodhana stared fixedly at him.

Sushasana and Shalya were standing on either side trying to calm him. Drona stood up and looked Suyodhana in the eye. 'I have served the Kuru empire for the last forty years. I have made you and your brothers the men that you are. I will be with you till the end.'

Sushasana and Shalya took Suyodhana to him, and after much cajoling, succeeded in making the two men embrace. A massive roar erupted in the tent.

Grandsire's plan was underway.

ABHIMANYU

I found Shikhandi in her tent.

'Sorry ma'am, I came to find the slayer of The Terrible One. Heard she was hiding in her tent, afraid of her own troops?'

She didn't look at me when she replied, 'It wasn't me, you know. Your father helped a little.'

I flopped on her bed and played around with some strewn trinkets. She was like an elder sister to me. I could count on her for anything. I was happy that she had killed Grandsire, well, almost killed him. He was still alive somewhere making his peace with his end.

The old man hadn't fought her after all. Just like Krishna had said. And looking at her in the tent, I only wondered why.

She was Drupada's eldest, and he had raised her like a son. 'It's no secret that women have always been tougher than men and my daughter will be the better of any bastard on a battlefield. These loins bring forth only the seed of warriors.' The speech was common knowledge now.

Her shoulders were round and manly, her chest nearly flat. So was her torso. She'd learned to wear her hair short and stand erect. To talk with a deep voice and listen without sympathy. Before the battle, her family had sworn to kill Grandsire Bhishma believing that as the head of the Kurus, he was responsible for all the humiliation caused to her sister Draupadi. No one dared question her presence on the battlefield for she was formidable in her own right. And Drupada's two-akshauhini-strong commitment to our cause left little room for argument.

'You both killed him. You know that.'

Again, she replied absent-mindedly, 'We all have our parts to play.'

'So, what now?'

'The war's not over, you know. There's a whole army on the other side.'

'True. All the others are alive too...Drona, Bhagadatta, Duryodhana.'

'Duryodhana?'

'That's what the bards are calling him these days. Clever, no? And Sushasana has become Dushasana. It seems their names are going to be ruined for posterity.'

'I don't think it'll mean anything to them.'

'I had thought you'd be happy for a change, Shikhandi. You're going to be remembered for this forever, you know. Up there with Parashurama, Drona and Father.'

'Forever, huh? I have no use for it. It's a lie we keep telling ourselves to divert our attention from the pointlessness of our sad little lives.'

'Relax, Shikhandi, what's wrong?'

'Nothing…nothing, okay. Just leave. I'll see you later.'

I left Shikhandi to her sulking and went back to my tent.

Grandsire had fallen. And I hadn't even been close. Back in the centre, waiting for my chance like everyone else. I had fought the old man before, though. It had been the first day of the battle. I took my chariot in front and called him out. He came leisurely. Obviously thinking I was a brat he could dispatch with one swift, unforgiving lesson. Four arrows to his breastplate later, I think he changed his opinion.

As his chariot rattled away with him unconscious on the planks, I turned around and looked for my father; to see if he had seen me defeat the greatest warrior in Bharatvarsha. He had. But he just stood on his chariot without an expression on his face and then turned his chariot to another fight. I had been used sparingly after that for the past ten days, mostly confined to the centre or placed at the back—given just a lick of the action, but never quite a whole morsel.

I think Father was behind it. He was taking advantage of being a senior member of the council by keeping me away from the front, like so many others boys of privilege.

I would have to do something about it.

My tent was small and sparsely decorated. More a mercenary's than a prince's. A large armoury dominated the room in the corner, and a bed with a writing table next to it was tucked to one side. I began looking through the mail strewn haphazardly on the table. A letter from Dwaraka—Mother's. She began, as usual, by berating the quality of attendants left to take care of the city. The palace is located near the sea, and without regular sweeping, sand infiltrates the wooden floors. Not one to be defeated by the laws of nature, Mother took it upon herself and several unwilling helpers to sweep the floors every second day.

Tough, as always.

My father, Arjuna, had taken my mother, Subhadra, a Yadava princess and Krishna's sister, as his fourth wife. He spent most of my childhood in Indraprastha, making short trips every few years to check on my progress. Then, when he was sent out into exile, I didn't see him for thirteen years. I never forgot him during those years, weaned as I was, on a steady diet of stories about his heroism. For Mother and Uncle Krishna, he could do no wrong. And the general ambition was that I would grow up and be just like him.

In the absence of my father, I was brought up by Uncle Krishna, my mother and Dwaraka herself, the new capital of the Yadava confederacy. The Yadava tribes had originally lived in and around the city of Mathura near the centre of Bharatvarsha. When Jarasandha, the king of Magadha, invaded the country with his hordes, we migrated and settled down on the edge of the western coast, eventually creating the kingdom of Anarta. The capital, of which, was a city by the sea that they called Dwaraka, meaning the 'City of Gates', to mark the Yadava exodus and serve as a reminder that in Yadava country everyone was always welcome. The Yadavas had done well here, ruling themselves in a unique fashion; as a confederacy of tribes where each tribe governed itself and its territories, but were also under the authority of a ruler, elected by a simple majority, currently Lord Ugrasena.

The confederacy had refused to take sides in the Kuru conflict, but offered their troops. The Kauravas had been able to secure the services of the elite Narayanis after the payment of a fat sum, while we were able to get troops of our own under Satyaki who, like Krishna, was close to my father and uncles.

I could smell sea salt in the parchment. All was well in Dwaraka, my mother had written. There had been a bit of a brawl a few days earlier between some female supporters of the Pandavas and some of the Kauravas. Mother had personally resolved the matter by pinching the ears of the chief parties. The matter was now forgotten and the womenfolk were back to crying in each other's arms about the folly of the male ego. The rest of the letter contained instructions on not to polish my armour and keep it dull to avoid undue attention, and replace its straps every second day.

There was also a letter from my wife. Her writing was small and demure, much like Uttaraa herself. The baby was fine, she said, it was kicking hard.

Our marriage was a strategic alliance to bind the Pandavas and the Matsyas. And we had gone about our business on the altar with little fuss. She was a simple soul. I had grown fond of her in the little time we had spent together before the war. One of these days, I'd write back to her at length.

For now, I scribbled a few sentences telling her I was fine, and turned in for the night.

Before I drifted off, I said a prayer for a place in the front tomorrow.

THE ELEVENTH DAY

YUDHISHTHIRA

A carrier pigeon came early in the morning. A wing was damaged and a leg sheared off. Lucky to be alive, this one. Evidently, Kaurava snipers were up last night. I unrolled the grubby piece of parchment while Vishaka tended to the wounded pigeon. A set of intricate symbols were scrawled on it, barely legible. It was a dangerous thing in these times. Handwriting can cost you wars. I sat at my desk and worked out the code Dhristadyumna had so meticulously created with Krishna.

This couldn't be right. I uncoded the symbols again. And again. I was almost tempted to ask Vishaka, peering from the corner of his eye, to try his hand at it.

'Jade Love Cloud.' The words were right. But it made no sense. 'Love' was the code word for me. Every evening after the war council in the Kaurava camp, Dhristadyumna had arranged for someone to inform us about the next day's plan. He never revealed his source, and we never asked him; the information had proved most reliable. At least until now.

I walked over to Dhristadyumna's tent. Krishna was there, cradled in a chair, playing with a peacock feather.

I showed them the parchment: 'I got today's message.'

Dhristadyumna nodded. The pigeons were supposed to be homed to him or me or Krishna. But only a few had come my way till now.

'What news?'

'Bizarre. actually. It says, "Jade Love Cloud".' I showed him the parchment, trying to act as nonchalant as possible. 'I think they may have cracked our code. It must be a ploy to make us arrange our forces in a way that suits them. What do the other agents say?'

The code had been created from an obscure text on gemstones and Dhristadyumna's childish imagination for intrigue. Each page of the book had been dedicated to a single stone, and we used this to refer to each day of the war. 'Jade' was page 11, which meant that the following actions would be perpetrated today. 'Love' was my name—for what reason, I will never know. And the final part of the message, 'Cloud' meant capture, as opposed to 'Rain' that meant kill and was seen more frequently.

This time, Krishna spoke, 'Believe it or not, brother, for once, all the spies are saying the same thing. The Kauravas want you as their guest—"Atithi Devo Bhava—the guest is God".' He smiled wickedly.

Dhristadyumna spoke softly, 'There are many messages flying around. Not all of them could be cracked overnight. But you have a point. Some of our codes may be compromised. I'll, er...look into it tonight. Let's plan to keep you on our side till then, right, brother? Come, the council is meeting now.'

We walked into the council tent and found everyone waiting for us. Drupada gave me a look that could have either meant 'I'm sorry for you' or 'I can't believe they want to capture you' or maybe both. He turned around and said matter-of-factly to Dhristadyumna, 'Shikhandi is not well. She won't join us in the council. We'll see her directly on the field.'

Bhima came to the point, 'Right, so everyone's here. The men need their orders. What's the plan?'

Dhristadyumna spoke, 'We have news from the other side that the main Kaurava thrust today will be directed towards Yudhishthira to...uh, capture him.'

Virata nodded his head. Krishna, still playing with his peacock feather paid no attention. Nakula and Sahadeva looked at each other as they always did when they didn't know how to react. Arjuna pursed his lips and shrugged. Bhima clucked his tongue and scratched himself.

Drupada, characteristically, spoke up, 'Yudhishthira? ...Are you sure, putra? Maybe it's a decoy.'

My father-in-law obviously had little regard for my ability to pose a threat to the Kaurava cause.

'There is no reason to assume that. It has also been confirmed that Drona is leading the troops and Radheya is entering the field today,' replied Dhristadyumna calmly.

The conversation teetered dangerously off the topic of my safety onto less relevant grounds.

Lord Drupada slapped his thigh, 'Ha! Finally! I propose we promptly dispatch him to the netherworld. Lead young Arjuna, Bhima and Satyaki with two akshauhinis and put him down for good.'

Dhristadyumna went purple and didn't know where to look. 'Uh, sire. I think our efforts today must involve protecting Yudhishthira. We have received the same information from multiple sources. It must be true.'

'Nonsense, boy, just go after Radheya. Leave Yudhishthira in the reserves with me and Virata. After all, what will we old folk do in the front, eh? We've had our day, now it's time for you to play.' He then turned to Bhima and beamed at him, 'That's poetry. I'm the next Valmiki, eh?'

I was about to glower at my father-in-law when I noticed Virata taking the trouble to do the same, though not so much on my behalf.

'Drupada,' he said in his nasal rasp, 'it would be nothing short of catastrophic if one of the key stakeholders in this conflict were captured and taken back trussed up like deer. My humble advice, leave the day's strategy to someone more competent.'

'Getting too old to play war, eh Virata?'

'They are better at it than me and you, I would imagine. Didn't you lose half your kingdom to Drona the last time you "played"?'

Dronacharya had, many, many years ago, made us mount an offensive against the Panchala king as part of our siege exercises in the academy. It was not authorized by any account, but we ran circles around the Panchala troops. Guru Drona, as chief negotiator, made Drupada cede half his territories to the Kurus, more specifically, to him.

If Drupada was ever upset about that incident, he never mentioned it. He married his daughter to us and years later, when the time came for us to wage war on the Kauravas, he was the first to offer his support. His only condition (apart from land and economic benefits) was a chance to kill Drona.

The embarrassed silence that follows any argument that has overreached its ambition made its presence felt now.

Chekitana, the youngest in our tent or any war council in the near vicinity bravely tried to change the subject.

'Sires, my spies tell me Prince Sushasana may be court-martialled for neglecting to protect Lord Bhishma.'

Drupada didn't hear him, 'He was able to because I had no great army, just a rabble of tribes. Let him try now. Let them all try. I'd even like to see you try.' He stood up and glared at Virata.

'Oh would you now? Sowing dissent minutes before a battle...just the way of the Panchalas.' Virata made to stand up.

I saw Krishna, but he just looked at me and grinned.

I had to say something, 'Lords, Lords! This is no time for anger, least of all over me. I agree, there are targets in this army to the Kauravas more valuable than myself—Arjuna, Bhima, Satyaki and even yourselves. There is a good chance of the information being false. And in any case, it would be selfish of me to even suggest that we hold back our troops for my protection.'

Drupada looked triumphantly at Virata, 'Ha! Thus speaks a king. You have nothing to worry about boy, just leave your hide to my Panchalas. Dhrista, take Bhima and Arjuna and bring Radheya's head on your shield.'

The peacock feather had failed to entertain Krishna, for he now got up and spoke, 'Uncle, while your suggestion is valid, coming as it does from the years of experience you've spent on battlegrounds, there is one element we haven't accounted for—Radheya himself. I know something of Radheya's tactics. He is not the kind of Maharathi to jump into the fray until he knows his enemy. Guru Drona will be a bigger threat today. Radheya's presence is merely meant to distract us. I believe that today Radheya will observe us from a safe distance waiting for the perfect moment to strike. And when he does, I can assure you it won't be Arjuna or Bhima, but a warrior with less ability.

It's well documented that he used the same approach in his campaigns against the Kamboja cavalry, the Girivraja mountain men and many others. He makes an appearance late in the battle and strikes a minor prince or corps commander but never a general or even an Atirathi. The next few days will see him increase his participation on the field, but for today, we have nothing to worry about.'

He turned and looked at me, 'As far as my eldest cousin is concerned, I do believe we should take adequate precautions. But keeping him in the reserve sends out two messages—one, that we know their plans, and the second, and most crucial in my opinion, that he is afraid of being taken.'

They were talking about me like I wasn't even in the room. I spoke up, just to remind them I was still here, and was as concerned about my safety as any of them, 'So, are you saying I should be up front?'

'No, no brother. While your eagerness to get killed is admirable, it won't serve our cause just yet.' Krishna smiled again, that wicked stretch of the lips.

Dhristadyumna spoke, 'You're right, Krishna. We'll place him in the centre, surrounded by our troops. Not too far ahead to be at risk, but not too far behind either. And, I have studied Radheya myself. As you rightly pointed out, I do believe he won't pose a direct threat today. Drona, on the other hand, deserves the full measure of our attention.'

There were nods of approval all around. Krishna smiled and looked at me. Drupada, sensing the argument slipping from his grasp, took a final shot. 'Well, don't say I didn't warn you when Radheya is riding our boys like a bull in heat.'

Krishna smiled back at him. 'With your blessings, sire, we

hope it never comes to that.'

Drupada settled back on his seat defeated and gestured to his son to continue.

Dhristadyumna said, 'I think today we will set up a strong perimeter around Yudhishthira on the field. He will be at the centre with the Panchala Corps lead by me and Shikhandi. Satyaki and the Matsya regiments will form a wall with the Yadavas. The rest of the men will be arranged around us. Bhima, Bhagadatta is your concern. Arjuna will lead the front line today with the Indraprastha Corps flanked by Nakula and Sahadeva and your Indraprastha regiments. Chekitana, your men got the worst of Grandsire yesterday, so we will hold them back in reserve.'

The council ended. Bali, the captain of our Indraprastha Corps, was waiting for us outside the tent. Arjuna debriefed him on his duties and he nodded and left. Bali was born mute but had been compensated adequately by the Lord in courage and battle awareness. His lieutenants had to learn sign language to serve under him and we had instituted special annual examinations to determine his field officers. It was a great honour for the young men of Indraprastha to belong to his batallion.

We made our way to the chariot park where our own arms lay. The park was abuzz with activity and the scent of dust disembowelled from the earth was intermingled with that of horses and humans. There were warriors from the south, dark and muscular; lithe and wiry men from the east and loud and boisterous ones from the north; all of whom found common ground on a whetstone or bowstring. Swords were being checked for sharpness. There were short blades that were accompanied with round shields, broadswords with blades as thick as a man's bicep, whip swords with elastic metal blades and snake-shaped blades with their wavy form. There were spears with supple wooden shafts and metal heads, maces with large domes being scrutinized for cracks alongside javelins that were being checked by armourers for sharpness and balance. There were weapons of makes and shapes I had never seen or heard of.

Bows were being flexed—simple ones made of bamboo, or more complex ones made of animal bone and metal. Bowstrings were being obtained with great haste. Strings made of vegetable fibre were preferred to those of animal fibre that could lose their suppleness if they got wet.

Man's capacity for killing his kin, and the imagination he was willing to put into it, never failed to surprise me.

At an almost reluctant pace, the armours were coming on. First, the breastplate made of iron or bronze, if the warrior could afford it, and hard wood or animal bone if he could not; then came the plates for the arms and shoulders. Thigh and shin armours were a luxury for most. Helmets would be strapped on at the battlefield. Protecting the faces, but more importantly, concealing fear in their shadows.

The first chariots began to leave for Kurukshetra, slowly, so as to not tire the horses.

Our Indraprastha Chariot Corps was the main fighting force from our own kingdom and consisted mainly of heavy chariots. Both the Kauravas and Pandavas were partial to these chariots that were borne by four horses and could carry multiple people depending on their girth. Each functioned like a mobile tower that anchored platoons of foot soldiers, shielding them, acting like a barricade from which they could launch sorties. Arjuna had decided that this was not a battle for lightly armoured chariots that could zip across the field. The battle, as he had envisioned it, would be a slow one with ground taken an inch at a time.

The chariots were almost exclusively manned by nobility with elephants. While elephants were treated as an object of reverence, prided by the general public for their ability to change the course of battles, the real celebrity belonged to the chariots. Boys all over Bharatvarsha dreamed of being chariot warriors. Playing in little box carts with visions of glory in their heads, with the weaker or younger ones relegated to serving as horsemen, or worse, foot soldiers. Men without a warrior lineage or backgrounds would spend vast sums of money trying to get admitted into the Indraprastha or Hastinapura gurukul and be a part of the Chariot Corps. A lot of them had found their way to the battlefield. Not many would leave.

As princes of the kingdom, it was assumed that we would tread the chariot's planks in war, and for the most part, it was an accurate assumption; except in the case of Bhima who had whimsically decided early on that he would fight on his feet, much to Guruji's and Grandsire's disgust. Eventually, as a compromise, Bhima learned the ways of battle from the less exalted vantage of a horse-drawn car, but was never very comfortable with its speed. As one of our two best fighters, he was often required to fight in different sectors during a single day. For that purpose alone, Bhima tolerated a chariot to take him in haste across the field. But once he had reached his destination he would always get down and fight like a common foot soldier.

The chariots trundled towards the field in greater mass now, warriors manoeuvred their vehicles closer to familiar faces. Mostly, a general understanding prevailed that no one would speak at this hour. The last few moments of silence before battle, maybe forever. The metallic cluck of chariot wheels played in the background along with the steady tramp of feet and the occasional trumpet of an elephant.

The Great War of Kurukshetra had a schedule to keep. Fighting began a few hours after dawn, when there was sufficient light for us to see who we were killing; and ended late in the afternoon, when the sky began to turn purple; which it did sooner these days given that it was nearing winter. There would be no breaks during this period and troops were generally called in from the centre or reserve to replace soldiers in the front line who had been fighting for too long.

Dhristadyumna came up to me with a young man who bore his features.

'Yudhishthira. This is my brother, Kumara. I'd, er, like him to flank your chariot today with Yudhamanyu and Uttamaujas.'

I had seen a few of his other brothers before. Uttamaujas and Yudhamanyu had been given strict instructions to stay close to me. They didn't talk much, and were brooding and intense most of the time, but polite enough when spoken to.

But this was a new brother. I wondered again, as I had countless times before, how many young princes had old Drupada spawned. The old goat's children practically populated half the battlefield.

I nodded and spoke to Kumara, 'So, youngster, are you ready to save my old hide in battle?'

He blushed.

'You won't run away chasing glory like your elder brother now, will you?' I said, playing the genial, experienced man of war.

Kumara went crimson, 'No, sir.'

I left Dhristadyumna, giving him some last instructions and

went to my chariot. I let my driver do a last-minute check on the wheels and the horses and began putting on my armour.

I heard Sahadeva's voice from behind me, 'Brother, could we talk?'

I nodded. My throat dry in anticipation of the battle.

'Look, I know...I mean, it's all well and good...but...'

'Spit it out, we don't have time.'

Sahadeva sighed, and began once more, 'I know that our allies are committed to us, brother. No one suspects them of anything but acting in the best interests, but over the past few days, a few of us have begun to, well, question...'

'Question what?'

Sahadeva sighed again. A melancholic figure, this brother of mine. 'Our men are being placed ahead every day and are getting butchered. The Matsyas and Panchalas are nowhere near the heat. Some of us are beginning to question Dhristadyumna's interests in running this army. Eventually, this could mean that we won't be able to have a say in the council. For the long term, I think we need to withhold as many troops as possible. To ward off any future pretenders to the throne who may take advantage of our weakened state. As our eldest, you should talk to Dhristadyumna about putting his troops in front flanked by the Matsyas and Yadavas.

'How badly off are we?'

'Conservatively, I'd say, our Indraprastha Corps could scrape together and field one akshauhini.'

'That's not too bad.'

'My sources tell me the Panchalas can account for an akshauhini and a few ankinis and the Matsyas around half an akshauhini comfortably. The Yadavas and Chekitana didn't come in with much to begin with, so after ten days they stand at a few ankinis each. Given that we started the battle with...'

He paused and looked, expecting me to play big brother and storm off in Dhristadyumna's direction to give him an earful.

At the beginning of the war, our coalition of forces stood at two akshauhinis from our kingdom of Indraprastha, two more from the Panchalas, an akshauhini from the Matsyas, another one from the Chedi kingdom under Chekitana and half an akshauhini from the Yadava Confederacy under Satyaki. Our remaining allies contributed a few ankinis each which added up to about half an akshauhini.

He had a point. But the last thing I wanted to do was accuse Drupada of holding back his troops and provoke him into leaving the battlefield for good.

'Well...it's too late to do anything today, Saha. Why couldn't you tell me this earlier?'

I was angry at the fact that all my brothers expected me to speak on their behalf, while they stood idly by in the shadow of my decision or indecision. That none of them would ever have to take responsibility for driving the Pandavas down to ruin except me.

Sahadeva looked down and said nothing.

I walked away without looking back.

RADHEYA

In my younger days, I would wear a pair of golden earrings and gold-plated armour to create a distinct look for myself so that kings would seek me out to duel. My desire to get myself killed, and my earrings soon led to a nickname from the troops: Karna—'the one with the earrings'.

Victory has the ability to twist facts and mould them into grotesque caricatures that people call legends.

My earrings and armour began to take on talismanic proportions, so I gave them away before people actually began to believe that the sum of the earrings and armour was greater than the warrior. No man should have to live with the burden of his own legend.

The troops still insisted on calling me Karna, though a little uncertainly now.

On the other side, it was happening to Arjuna. I had heard his bow was being called Gandiva, or 'Conqueror of the Earth', by the troops who had begun to believe the bow was indestructible and its wielder invincible.

A misconception I would soon clear.

I began my pre-battle routine by inspecting my arrows. Today, and for most of my killing career, my quiver was home to Kshurupras with their sharp razor-like heads, Vatsadantas with heads shaped like calf-teeth, broad-headed Anjalikas and my old reliables, Ardhachandra, crescent-shaped arrow heads. All of these were bronze-tipped.

Apart from these, I also carried a separate quiver with iron-tipped arrows (which the army had named Shakti, meaning 'strength'). Battles were decided not by courage but metals these days, so I kept my iron arrows close at hand, using them sparingly, only on kings.

All seven-odd akshauhinis that were left of our army were spread out in front of me. I saw the chariot of Sushasana canter into view and motioned my charioteer towards it. He was a sight, the great lubber—short and muscular with thick ringlets of hair covering his face. His bronze armour had the face of a lion embossed on it. He gave me an embarrassed grin and shrugged his shoulders. Drona had put him in the reserve today and told him not to show his face for the entire day.

'So, Sushasana, live to fight another day, eh?' I sympathized.

Sushasana grinned back nervously. 'Live, yes. Fight, not so much.' He pushed his hair off his eyes. 'But it's a big day for you. Time to show them what stable-boy hands can do, no?'

This made me laugh, 'The stable teaches many things, Sushasana. Cleaning shit, most of all.'

The conch announcing the commencement of battle sounded at a distance. Sushasana bowed mock-solemnly to me, 'All yours, stable boy. Come back in one piece.'

My chariot rode towards the front. I heard Sushasana's voice from the back, 'And clean some of that shit!'

I smiled to myself. Today, we had planned after much deliberation, that my Anga troops and Bhagadatta's elephant brigade supported by Shakuni would lead and cut through to Yudhishthira. Once we had cleared the way, Drona would slingshot in and pick up my brother. Not my usual style, but since yesterday, there was no other choice.

The conch blew again. It was Drona's, I could tell from its refrain. Then there was a blast of conches from the other side.

I took in the sight of our army. Thousands of battle standards hung limply on top of their chariots. The battle standard was another symbol of the puffed vanity of our nobility. A banner that flew on top of chariots of the nobility with symbols that 'represented the noble value of the house'. In short, it told everyone on the field whose chariot it was. And if you didn't have one, God help you. The nobility wouldn't even approach you for a fight. My own was an elephant rope that mahouts used to secure the girth of an elephant. It was meant to depict my position as protector of the Kuru princes...a little tacky perhaps, but Suyodhana's choice.

A sense of gloom still pervaded the ranks. Grandsire's mere presence had put strength into these boys' arms. Without him, it was as if they had woken from a trance, realizing that without Grandsire they were responsible for their own lives. They would be careful today. Maybe even hesitate a little.

I made my way to the front. My chariots had been arrayed in a neat line behind Bhagadatta's heavyweights. I looked left and right for him when a coconut landed on my chariot floor, causing my poor charioteer to invoke his ancestors in fright. I looked upwards and saw Bhagadatta happily munching away, feeding Supritika at the same time.

''Bout time you came ... Thoo...was worried sick. Thought I'd have no one to share the glory with...'

I lowered my eyes and gave him the smartest namaskaram I had. The old fire breather still insisted on riding into battle on his beast without a mahout, though no mahout could have possibly handled Supritika. I left the two of them to their appetite and went over to my corps commander. He squinted as he saw me approaching; his real green eye shining, while his fake emerald one sparkled merrily in its socket.

'Good day to die, Radheya.'

Narsimha was the only member of my personal staff who was allowed to address me by my first name. He had been with me throughout, this green-eyed ogre, and I saw him rise from a foot soldier to cavalryman to brigade commander and now corps commander. I had even been with him years ago, when a Kamboja rider put a lance through his eye during a charge, and returned the favour for him by shooting down his attacker.

Loud jeers from behind interrupted my answer. Shakuni was arranging his Kamboja light cavalry. Narsimha looked at them disdainfully and spat.

I surveyed my chariots and took my place ahead of them. I didn't like commanding elephants as they were too unpredictable. I wasn't too fond of infantry either as it required infinite patience to handle them. Chariots were my joy. I have often believed that human beings were never meant to go fast because speed brings out the savage in us. And in a chariot, quickening towards the enemy, crying your throat hoarse in the heat of war, is when you truly discover the part of you that you've been brought up to hide.

The Pandava army spread out in front of me. It appeared they were favouring an aggressive stance today as they were in a Krauncha formation, so called because the troops in front were arranged in the shape of a crane's beak. I could make out Arjuna's battle standards with the image of Hanuman, the monkey god, flanked by Nakula and Sahadeva, but there was no sign of my eldest cousin.

Our own formation was a basic Sakata or box—a broad arrangement of no great imagination which could be equally effective in offense or defense. We would lead with Bhagadatta's elephants and once they had punched a hole in the centre, my chariots supported by infantry would follow.

The troops waited anxiously for the signal to charge. It is impossible to remember what is going through your mind in the last minutes before a battle. Most soldiers don't even notice that they've pissed in fright. Their heads throb. Their breath quickens. And more than a prayer for their life, they pray for the wait to get over, for the killing to begin, or the dying.

A final conch blew.

The trumpets began to cry and the drums started. Cymbals crashed and fifes sounded over the deep bass thud of human and animal footsteps. Bhagadatta's elephants walked ponderously towards the Pandava lines while Arjuna's chariots gathered pace from the other side. I nodded to Narsimha who gave the sign, and my chariots made their way at a safe distance behind Bhagadatta's troop.

Another peal of trumpets sounded and the elephants, goaded by their mahouts, increased their speed. All except Supritika who continued unhurried. I began to lose sight of them as the dust temporarily blinded us. 'Steady!' I heard Narsimha cry and cough shortly after. The sound of metal clashing grew louder as we neared the line. I saw Supritika, now among our chariots, still in no hurry.

A sharp cry broke my reverie. A horseman came thundering through the dust and hacked wildly at me with a sword. I avoided his swipe and let the chariots behind me butcher him.

My chariot trundled into the front slowly. My foot soldiers came up from behind and formed a wall around the chariots allowing us to move at a genial pace and bring out our bows. I spotted a chariot warrior heading in our direction. He was just at the right distance for my first kill. I fixed an arrow and fired.

And missed him.

Narsimha, protecting my right, coughed and spat into the ground. 'I've seen virgins on honeymoons less eager, Radheya...'

I cursed him for the fool he was and nocked another arrow. This time, I tore out the warrior's jugular.

Our elephant front had slowed to a halt.

Platoons of Pandava infantry with 15-foot-long spears had positioned themselves around the elephants to prevent them from charging. The elephants now just stood like towers, swaying their necks eerily. Supritika strolled in and was promptly surrounded by the Pandava infantry. I could make out Bhagadatta. He stood on his howdah and took in the panorama. Then bringing out his trumpet, he blasted three short, angry whistles. Supritika shook her head and charged, the spears breaking through her armour and into her body. The other elephants followed her, some successfully, but quite a few impaled by the spears.

This was my sign. Narsimha sounded the conch and we went in behind the elephants. No Yudhishthira in sight. Naturally he wouldn't be up front, but I hoped he wouldn't be cowering in the reserve either.

I could make out Bhima's broad bulk in the distance furiously directing his infantry towards an elephant. He was in a silver-coloured chariot and for once, his mace was not in his hand; a bow was in its place. One of Suyodhana's younger brothers, Vivimsati, saw the same and probably fancied his chances. With a couple of well-placed arrows, he shot Bhima's horses. A third arrow took him on the shoulder. Enraged, Bhima picked up his mace and ran towards Vivimsati's chariot. An overhead blow broke the horse's neck and another swing deprived the chariot of a wheel while Vivimsati looked on in disbelief. He jumped out of his chariot before it collapsed and retreated towards another chariot, hacking wildly away at the air and an imaginary enemy. Bhima, heaving and grunting, shouted at him loudly to come back and fight like a man.

On my right, his brother Nakula was having problems of his own containing his uncle, Shalya, who mowed down his infantry guard with arrows. To his credit, Nakula made a fighting retreat, giving time for someone else to take his place. Smart. On a bad day, I would think carefully before taking on Shalya.

A group of battle standards with the insignia of a fish lay ahead of me. They were the Matsyas, led by Virata. Our chariots clashed and I saw Virata manoeuvre his chariot in front of me. The old fool. I put an arrow in my bow, and shot him full in the chest. He reeled backwards but his armour prevented any real damage. A couple of infantrymen formed a protective fence around him and I fired arrows deliberately at their unprotected faces.

Virata had regained his composure by now and hurled a javelin which I dodged easily. Another one nearly went through my charioteer. He picked up his bow again and started attacking me with arrows, most of which were pathetically off mark. This would be too easy. I began whistling as I calmly picked up an arrow and released it. It smacked him on his shoulder, the next one pierced his thigh, and a third one cut beautifully across his left bicep.

The Matsya contingent tried to rally around old Virata to protect him, but Narsimha and the chariots held them off. I put an arrow through the old king's helmet and took out the next arrow with the intention of putting it through his throat. A loud trumpet interrupted my careful shot. An elephant, riderless and stuck through with javelins and arrows, came lumbering through my fight crushing a few chariots in its wake. In the confusion, Virata escaped and the Matsya ranks closed in behind him.

A chance to take out a member of the Pandava war council did not come easily. I was furious and vented my anger on the Matsyas, killing as many as I could before their reinforcements arrived. When they did, I moved behind and let Narasimha take over.

From the looks of it, Supritika and the surviving elephants had nearly touched the centre of the Pandava forces in their charge and were being contained successfully this time.

Yudhishthira was being sorely missed. I told my charioteer to go towards the centre.

ABHIMANYU

My orders were to take charge of a detachment of the reserve corps under Shikhandi. I was to be tucked away safe, a half yojana or so, from the front. I thought of going and protesting to Dhristadyumna, but it was nearly battle hour so I resigned myself to reporting for the reserves, at least temporarily.

Father was behind this, I was sure. Hiding me from the fight.

Shikhandi met me near the Reserve Corps. She was elegant as usual, wearing a garland of white lotuses over her white armour and cream-coloured dhoti.

She started, 'Listen, I'm sorry about yesterday. I just hate all the attention.'

'Hate it? So soon? If I were you, I'd be hiring bards by now, not that that's going to stop them. Tomorrow Uttaraa will be asking me if you really are eight feet tall. You're famous, sister. Live with it, because it's going to live a lot longer than you.'

'What if I don't want to be famous?

'What do you want then?'

She exhaled and looked out at the battle in front.

'I want to be left alone.'

There was sadness in the words; an invitation to observe its surface, but not explore its depths. She had spent her life fighting her father's battles, being a better man than any of the men. And now, that was how everyone was going to remember her.

She turned to me with a sly smile, 'I know what you want, Abhimanyu. A name; a following; a page or two dedicated to you in a book. Maybe even a whole book. A life that generations of children will learn by rote, and remember as adults when they are vulnerable. I have lesser demands.'

I didn't appreciate the sarcasm, 'Look, whether you like it or not, you've been part of something that is going to be spoken about for many yugas, hopefully. Get used to it.'

She looked far away into battle lines drawing closer like storm clouds. 'I suppose you're right. I hope you get your glory, Abhimanyu. You can have mine too.'

'Thank you, generous Lady Shikhandi. Alms for the glory seeker?'

She continued looking into the distance but laughed, 'You'll get yours some day. Perhaps more than your father. But a word of advice: you won't get it back here with us.'

I rolled my eyes at her and she gave an understanding smile.

I made my way into the reserve division and waited.

YUDHISHTHIRA

It was a beautiful morning. The sky was a happy blue, undisturbed by clouds. A light wind was blowing, the kind that makes its presence felt without seeking your attention. The earth, it appeared, was a satisfied spectator to our little games.

The day's battle hadn't started well for us. Bhagadatta's monsters had scattered our army like wood shavings in the wind. Reports from the front indicated that Bhima was falling short of men to contain them with. It was a good opportunity to recommend that one of the Panchala princes and a regiment or two be sent to buttress my brother. After much reluctance, Dhristadyumna agreed and Drupada insisted that he be allowed to lead the regiment, having heard that Virata had also insisted on making his way up ahead.

Drupada didn't have to go too far, however, as I saw Supritika, a little distance ahead, tearing off the head of an unfortunate chariot warrior spraying his gore across the men around her. She was a sight. A monster of a she-elephant whom nature had chosen to endow with four tusks in place of two. Supritika was clad from tusks to toenails in expensive silver-coloured iron armour that could finance the services of an ankini of mercenaries. Her iron helmet had Bhagadatta's Pragjyotisha lightning bolt battle standard etched on it and was lined with large iron spikes. While most elephants were required not to wear much armour on their legs as it restricted their movements, Bhagadatta also insisted on providing Supritika with iron leggings.

From what I had seen in the past ten days, it didn't slow her down much.

Drupada and his regiment of Panchala chariots wheeled around and headed towards Supritika's flank. A troop of Kaurava chariots saw them coming and intercepted them before they were able to surprise her. Drupada emerged from the fray, got off his chariot and called out, 'Bhagadatta, come down and fight if you have the balls.'

He went on for a few moments, raving like a man on bhang.

Drupada took out his sword—the Naraka dristhi, which means 'Vision of Hell'. Thirty-five inches of good Panchala iron that the king had exhausted his vocabulary describing. Iron was the future, he said, and Panchala would be at the heart of the arms trade when this war was done. As part of his alliance benefits, he was to secure the kingdom of Anga which he believed to be a potentially great centre of iron production.

Bhagadatta stood up and yawned.

He bent over from his howdah and said something to his beast. She lowered herself to let her master off. A small circle was created by soldiers of both armies with Bhagadatta and Drupada in the centre. From my perch on the chariot, I peered from a distance into the makeshift ring, sharing everyone's morbid curiosity.

He looked at least a hundred, and I suspect that wasn't too far off the mark. But he certainly didn't act his age. Palace gossip in Pragjyotisha put his consumption of liquor to be at least twelve jars of unwatered sura in the day. That and two women in his chambers at night were offered as explanation for the wrinkle lines that circuited merrily across his face.

Both men squared off each other and then with quickness I never knew he had, Drupada flattened his sword and thrust it into Bhagadatta's armour.

Except Bhagadatta wasn't there.

The old king of Pragjyotisha had learned to wield his sword from an obscure mountain tribe in Chin beyond the mountains of the north. He favoured a short sword, nearly half the size of Drupada's, along with the sceptre he used to goad Supritika. His stance was not classical and he kept weaving from one direction to another, never still for more than a moment. Drupada thrust unsuccessfully again, and hacked to his right and left. Bhagadatta danced out of range and darted back in. A few more inconclusive chops followed and then a desperate lunge. Bhagadatta, moving with the reflexes of a much younger man, twisted away from the blow, planted himself on one knee and presented a backhander of his own, slicing upwards, and cutting Drupada across his armpit which was unprotected by his armour. An instant later he had rotated on his knee and delivered a sharp blow with his pommel to the back of Drupada's knee, taking him off his feet.

Drupada lay on his back with Bhagadatta's sword at his neck. The fight was over, it appeared. All that remained was for Bhagadatta to end it formally. Instead, he lifted the Naraka Drishti, which was lying close by, and proceeded to snap it viciously across his knee, looking into Drupada's eyes all the time. Drupada squirmed and tried to get up and found Bhagadatta's sword back at his neck.

Before he was able to strike, a troop of Panchalans forced their way into the fighting circle, distracting Bhagadatta. Drupada squirmed out from under him, and for the second time in the last few moments, displayed agility I never thought him capable of. He escaped to join his Panchala troops.

Bhagadatta climbed back on Supritika and we heard his voice from atop the beast, 'Next time bring a sword to a fight, not a walking stick, you senile fool.'

I went around and found my father-in-law sitting on the back of a chariot in a terrible mood.

Being on the losing side of a fight and alive was never quite acceptable to Kshatriyas. And given that my family included Bhima and Arjuna, I didn't have much experience in consoling defeated warriors. I left him to the care of his troops.

ABHIMANYU

The messenger galloped into our midst and nearly fell off his horse.

'Bha...Bhaga...'

I gestured to him to calm down and catch his breath.

'Lord Bhagadatta's elephants have been pushed back. Lord Radheya is in front, supported by the Kambojas.'

'And my father?'

'Sorry, my Lord, I'm not fully sure...some soldiers believe

he has penetrated the Kaurava formation.'

'Is that all?'

'Yes, my Lord, er...also the commander-in-chief believes it is too early to commit reserves and requests you to stay your ground.'

I dismissed the messenger. Leaving me in the reserves while Bhagadatta and Radheya slaughtered our armies demonstrated Dhristadyumna's lack of vision. My place was up ahead. It made no sense to waste me in the back with the rest of this unambitious lot. I looked around me. The men stood listlessly in the sun. A few kings on their chariots were chatting with their staff. No one seemed concerned about the war going on in front.

There was no future in this.

I told my charioteer, an old hand who insisted on treating me like a favourite nephew and went by the name of Sumitra, to take us forward.

I looked back at Shikhandi commanding the reserves. She saw me breaking rank, but looked away.

I reached the centre of our army fairly quickly and located Uncle Yudhishthira looking nervously out front. The Pragjyotisha elephants had retired, their place being taken by rows of chariots. Uncle drummed the front of his chariot. The anxiety was evident in his eyes. He was not meant for this, my uncle. With his slight pot belly and dreamy eyes, he looked more like a poet than a warrior. He was my eldest uncle but his general look of helplessness made him seem like the youngest.

'Aren't you supposed to be in the back?' he asked distractedly.

I nodded but didn't say anything, looking ahead at Radheya's chariots. I could spot him at a distance. They spoke well of him...a dangerous man on the field. But I could see nothing that set him apart. He wore a plain grey armour and white dhoti. A dark stubble and unimpressive features made him look even more like a common foot soldier.

Dhristadyumna approached us and spoke to Yudhishthira, 'Why is he here?'

Yudhishthira shrugged and said, 'Perhaps he wants to slake his thirst for blood a little.'

'I have no shortage of men wanting to die. When his turn comes, I'll be glad to send him.'

Dhristadyumna then turned to me. 'Go back. You'll get your chance soon.'

Yudhishthira gave me an apologetic half-grin, ending the conversation.

I turned around and headed back a little distance.

Then I told Sumitra to stop. Without my asking, he spurred the chariot around towards the front discreetly, away from my commander-in-chief or my uncle. As usual, he was the only one who understood me.

The Kaurava chariots were moving slowly, protected by platoons of foot soldiers grinding down everything in their path. I fixed my gaze on an isolated chariot on the far right and headed towards it. He was a young nobleman, not much older than me, wearing bronze armour and a lapis-lazuli-encrusted helmet and earrings. I reached back and pulled out a short bow that I used for high-power close-range shots. Two arrows took down his battle standard that had the sun inscribed on it and punctured his breastplate. He didn't flinch and came at me with a few shots of his own, nearly taking off Sumitra's head with one. I felt a sharp twinge of pain flit across my right arm as an arrow missed its mark. Another one cracked my bow, nearly taking a finger. Sumitra rushed our chariot into him to prevent him from taking another shot. I picked up a short sword and shield from my chariot armoury and jumped off.

A foot soldier with a spear lunged at me. I avoided the blow and thrust the sword into his neck. There was no time to give him a clean death. I walked quickly towards the nobleman. He got off his chariot and ran at me with a long two-handed blade swinging downwards. I dodged the blow comfortably. Good with a bow, but a pedestrian slasher with the sword. I would wear him out.

He hacked and thrust at me, shattering my shield with one huge strike and jarring my left arm. I continued to move around, not committing myself to a thrust or swipe, letting him tire out. Sure enough, after a little while, his swings became rounder and less focused. He was finished. I side-stepped a half-hearted lunge and smashed my pommel into his back. He fell down heavily. Three soldiers armed with swords came to thwart my kill. I hacked off the first one's hand as he thrust towards me. I caught the second one in the belly as he tried to swing his sword overhead. The third soldier was in two minds whether to attack or not, so I obliged by grasping his hand holding the sword and struck heavily on his neck. In the meantime, the nobleman had crawled to his chariot and was trying to catch his breath.

I walked over to him.

'Whom do I have the honour of killing?' He had fought well.

'Paurava of Purushapura. Make it quick.'

His charioteer ran towards me, arms flailing and was impaled by my sword for his efforts. Paurava spat at me, 'He was defenceless, you bastard.'

I lifted him up by his neck and met the hatred of his gaze with an equal measure of solemnity.

'No one here is defenceless.'

I cracked his nose with my pommel and ripped off his helmet for his insolence. He had long hair by which I held him and hit him several times in the face till he was senseless. I cut off the straps of his armour and dragged him back to my chariot by his hair. The men cheered while he pawed at my hands weakly.

A javelin flew past me from behind. Someone wanted my attention. I turned around and saw a chariot sporting the battle standard of a peacock. Its owner stepped off and spoke with a harsh, guttural voice.

'Let the boy go. Fight me.'

I cut open Paurava's neck and left him to find his end. The new arrival was a man of moderate build. He carried a beautiful concave shield which had a peacock emblem on its face and was bordered by rows of little bells. I picked up a small shield lying on the ground and walked slowly towards him.

'As you wish, Lord...?'

His face remained expressionless.

'Jayadratha of Sindhu.'

He dropped his guard for an instant, and I took a chance and rushed at him, slamming into his chest with my right shoulder. He fell back, winded. I cut at him, but he rolled backwards and got back on his feet. I prepared for his attack and he whirled in with a cry of anger and slashed long fluent strokes in the air. I avoided his blows and fought back by delivering two simultaneous blows—a descending chop followed by a thrust.

He escaped both and managed to find my skin with his sword. I lunged at him, and he thrust his sword savagely at my shield.

It went straight through.

I took a step back. The sword stuck its tongue out at me from within the shield. We both stopped, surprised. I silently thanked the Gods for cheap shields and expensive iron blades. Jayadratha decided against retrieving his sword and with impossible dignity turned his back to me and walked to his chariot.

I stood there gaping like a fool at my shield. Had I won the duel or lost it? A javelin cast at me for the second time in the day broke my reverie. It missed me by inches and fixed itself into the mud a little distance away. I walked over and picked it up. It was made of iron with gold work on the shaft and a large blue stone in the centre of its blade—an expensive weapon to squander. Its owner approached from afar upon his chariot.

I picked up the javelin and faced my third duel of the day. The shaft was heavy, but had a beautiful balance to it. A killing man's weapon. I took lazy aim and hurled it in the general direction of my aggressor. It went cleanly through his charioteer, pinning him onto the chariot face.

A round of cheers greeted this act. I looked back to see Shikhandi beaming at me. So the reserve contingent had finally come out of hiding.

RADHEYA

The boy had balls. Great, big ones.

He was Arjuna without the thin moustache and grey lines in his hair. He wore golden armour and a red dhoti bordered with gold, an obvious attempt to be noticed on the battlefield.

I was interested to see how he would take on Shalya and was pleased with what I saw—a perfect throw, square into the unfortunate charioteer. The impact rattled the chariot, nearly throwing Shalya off. As soon as he was able to stop the shaking vehicle, he picked up a large iron mace and went hunting for the boy.

Abhimanyu didn't seem overly impressed and was ready to take him on with a broken short sword when Bhima made an entry.

My chariots had punched through the Pandava formation. They had virtually no elephants to face us with and only a handful of chariots. But their foot soldiers fought with every possible weapon they could get their hands on and every inch on dust was hard-earned. I had never seen this degree of intensity on a battlefield. It was almost as if the last ten days had made the conflict personal to each one of them. No life was given easily, nor taken. We butchered our way slowly to the middle, stopping at places just to remove the heaps of carcasses that blocked our path. In some places, the troops spoke of walking through ankle-deep blood with carcasses floating past them like lotuses in a pond.

When we finally reached what we believed to be the centre, I saw Abhimanyu showing Shalya his skill with the javelin. Shalya came after him with a mace when he was interrupted by a bellowing Bhima. There stood the great oaf, ruining a good fight. Bhima had a word with Abhimanyu and sent the boy back into their lines. He cracked his fingers and brought out a leather sack from his chariot and removed a thick iron mace from it. It was a beauty, with gold and hemp interweaves and an iron head as broad as a bull's skull.

On the face of it, they weren't evenly matched. Bhima loomed over Shalya like an oak and was twice as wide. But Shalya had a wiry strength about him and a reputation for being the best mace fighter in the north.

And Bhima was not going to let some glory-happy brat spoil his chance to test it.

They began circling each other warily. Neither of them wanted to give any indication of their styles. Bhima prodded his mace into Shalya's face and it was brutally struck down. Bhima appeared surprised by the power that went into the blow, and circled a little more cautiously. Shalya swung viciously but found his arc uninterrupted by Bhima's bulk. Now it was his turn to be surprised. Bhima's technique, I knew for a fact, relied more on speed than his strength. His mass was simply a decoy for his quickness.

They continued circling, looking for an opening in the steady anticipation that only veterans possess. After some moments, Shalya struck. It was another downward swing, but this time the mace went down faster. Bhima stopped the blow and pushed back, then using his weapon like a battering ram, hit Shalya full in the chest. Shalya fell down but rolled back on his feet without wasting time. He went after Bhima with a series of attacks, striking him repeatedly on the arms and shoulders. Dazed from Shalya's onslaught, Bhima retreated. Shalya came whirling in again, finishing with a devastating upper cut, which was sidestepped. The momentum behind the stroke made Shalya lose his balance and Bhima struck his adversary's shoulder with all the strength he possessed. Shalya spun and fell on his face. He spent a few moments on the ground, trying to catch his wind, and got up slowly. Bhima let him take his time.

This was no longer war. It was something more sacred, a personal test. Shalya tottered up to his feet. Bhima was waiting. The pace of the contest slowed. They took fewer shots now, waiting for the other to make a mistake. This continued for some time till both were drained of all energy.

Then Bhima planted his feet firmly on the ground and swung at Shalya, pounding his chest with a blow that could have lifted a full-grown buffalo off its feet. Shalya didn't flinch. He stood on the spot and returned the blow to Bhima's shoulder. They stood in their places and continued hammering away, one after the other.

Finally, Shalya fell.

Bhima dropped to a single knee, sobbing with relief.

YUDHISHTHIRA

Midday saw silhouettes of crows and vultures circling leisurely overhead against the stark canvas of the sky.

Shalya lay still on the ground and all of us held our breaths. Bhima stood up, leaning heavily on his mace. He tore off his helmet and roared.

Two men lifted Shalya by his arms and he twitched violently as they carried him back to his chariot. So the old king was alive. For how long, remained the question. The chariot made its way back into the Kaurava lines. As soon as it was out of sight, Radheya's Anga chariot archers fired straight into us and charged, supported by their infantry.

Our men in front were killed almost instantly and the men behind them wavered. Dhristadyumna sent a squadron of chariots to the front line to bolster them. I kept an eye out for Bhima. I had last seen him hobble into his chariot, an arrow clinging stubbornly to his leg.

A great clamour went up on the far right. The Anga chariots had opened their ranks. And before we knew it, our front was being run over by horsemen. I went up to Dhristadyumna, who was talking to Shikhandi, who had come in with the reserves.

'Shakuni, I'm certain. Kambojas…hawk feathers on the spear shaft, see. '

'I'm on it.'

Dhristadyumna saw me and snapped, 'You go back.'

His anger stung me. I didn't say anything but moved my chariot rapidly in the direction of the fight. From the corner of my eye, I saw Dhristadyumna throw up his arms and turn back to the fight.

Did he really think I needed to be protected? That little strip of a general. I had seen my share of battles and didn't need his expert opinion on my safety. Just because I didn't like killing, didn't mean I couldn't fight.

I was thirteen the day we began our weapons' training at Hastinapura. Innocent of skill and the patience required to master it. Until then, we had practised basic drills with wooden weapons. From that day, it would be different.

We were taken to the training pit before sunrise. The pit was surrounded by long wooden galleries that contained metal shields, swords and maces that were old and battleworn. I remember Nakula, Sahadeva and me along with the Kuru boys looking at these weapons with practised apathy. Inside, we were shaking with excitement. The preferred subject of fantasy every night for years was finally in front of us.

Barely out of infancy, Arjuna and Bhima had been discovered as prodigies with the bow and mace. From then on, they attended special private classes with Guru Drona himself and we never saw them except for a day or two in a month. For less gifted warriors like me or my brothers standing in a row beside me, this was our first glimpse of a world we had only heard about in the occasional excited ramblings of our two more fortunate ones.

The training pit is a cruel place for the egos of young boys, and it soon became evident that I was useless with the bow or sword. My skills with the axe or mace were marred by my inability to lift them beyond a few inches off the ground. The visions of glory fled from my mind overnight. I began to hate early mornings and found solace in books and the company of scholars.

After a particularly intensive session with swords where I had been defeated roundly by a boy much smaller than me, I flung down my blade. The entire pit fell silent. To disrespect weaponry was sacrilege here, where we offered prayers to our weapons before and after training. The instructor came up to me without any anger on his face and punched me hard on the jaw. It was afternoon when I woke up. The sword lay next to me on the ground. Training was over. But I had been left behind at the pit. Slowly I came to my feet and patted the dust off my clothes and made to walk back to the barracks.

I had only taken a few steps when I heard a deep voice call out my name.

It was Guru Drona. I lowered my eyes and bowed my head as he approached. 'I heard you didn't treat your weapons kindly today, putra,' he said softly.

I didn't know what to say so I kept my head lowered, and prepared for another blow.

'It wasn't the right thing to do. But I think you already know that.'

I looked at him, seeking sarcasm in his eyes, finding none.

'Putra, being a warrior does not come naturally to everyone. You have to find what comes to you.'

But I am born a Kshatriya...to fight,' I pleaded.

'We're all born to do certain things, but not necessarily the right circumstances in which to do them. In life, we have to fulfil both—the expectations we have been born into and those we have made for ourselves.'

I didn't quite understand him and it must have shown. His beard stretched into a smile.

'Become a warrior. But don't let it become you.'

I remembered those words as my chariot rumbled towards the Kambojas. They were pulverizing our ragged front, pushing into our lines with their enormous steeds.

I lifted a stabbing spear and balanced it between my thumb and forefinger. I didn't have the necessary rage to handle a mace or the serene calm to handle a bow, but I was equipped with enough nervousness to poke at anything approaching me with intent.

My chariot went to the front of the line and our infantry began rallying around me. A lancer charged at me and I went on my knee to the chariot floor and stuck out my spear, jabbing unsuccessfully at him as he passed. Two riders charged at me from either side. One hacked at my chariot umbrella as he went, nearly dislodging the battle standard, and the other struck a glancing blow at the side of my chariot and sped away. I set my spear aside and picked up a javelin which I threw with all my strength at an oncoming horseman. It went through his chest and felled him from his horse. A few horsemen came up at a canter, but a wall of infantry gathered around me and beat them off.

Behind us, Shikhandi had gathered the chariot warriors of the reserves. With mechanical precision, they took out their quivers and began peeling off arrows from behind us into the Kamboja horsemen.

Abhimanyu was here despite Dhristadyumna's instructions. And he was doing magnificently. He didn't even need to stop to look where he was firing, but still managed to find a victim for most of his arrows. Shikhandi was more deliberate. Marking her targets carefully, stalking them till she felt confident of a kill. Bhima was back on his feet and stringing a bow impatiently. We moved ahead, recovering ground slowly, pushing back the Kamboja horsemen.

Some moments later a trumpet was heard. A row of infantry with leopard skins draped around their armour marched in to take the place of the remaining horsemen. Shikhandi looked at me and raised her eyebrows. The new leopard-skinned arrivals were Suyodhana's personal guard. But to the best of our knowledge he was nowhere near this part of the field.

We were right.

Four chestnut-coloured mares drawing a white chariot with a battle standard that bore the emblem of a sacrificial fire came into view. Clad in a simple white armour with no embellishments, and holding a large, white war bow was Guru Drona. The leopard skins took a step in front together and swung their large double-handed battleaxes in a perfectly synchronized upward thrust. Then another step, and once again, a thrust. Our infantry stepped back, unable to counter the savageness of their assault. Drona and a row of chariots came up slowly behind the Leopard Warriors. Dhristadyumna was already behind me telling me to get away, but it was too late. Guru Drona saw me and charged his chariot into our lines, crushing some of his own soldiers in the process.

I took up a javelin and threw it at my Guru and followed it with another. Both went horribly off mark. I readied my stabbing spear and planted my knee on the chariot in the approved stance for meeting a charging foe, when another chariot went hurtling past me bearing a Panchala standard. It was Kumara.

The fool.

I shouted at him to turn back, but he didn't even look at me. Instead he drew an arrow and fired. The next thing I saw was my guru with an arrow plunged into his chest. Kumara fired another arrow which nicked Guruji's arm and then, growing in confidence, assaulted him with a barrage of three arrows in quick succession. Where was this skill coming from? And why hadn't anyone seen it before? Guruji reeled in his chariot and nearly fell off. His charioteer made to retreat. Our boys let out a big cheer and Kumara was distracted for a few moments.

That was enough for Guruji to lift his bow and fire.

Blood and saliva dribbled out of Kumara's mouth. And then his head fell off. A crescent-headed arrow was stuck on the chariot behind Kumara's while his head rolled aimlessly in the mud.

Kumara's body sagged to the chariot floor and twitched till life found its escape. I looked at Dhristadyumna and found everyone was doing the same. He lowered his head, conscious of the attention, then looked straight ahead and shouted: 'Shore up the line, bring the chariots in front.'

The men obeyed and Kumara's death was soon out of the minds of most, but it stayed with me for the rest of the day. To watch your younger brother being killed before you…it was the thing that frightened me most. I tried not to think how Dhristadyumna would be feeling.

I pushed towards the back while the chariots formed a line up ahead to meet Guruji. A loud crash took me by surprise and I realized that Guruji was already attacking. He was ringed by the Leopard Infantry and supported by a wedge of chariots. Together, they tore apart our front and plunged in.

Shikhandi was the first in Guruji's path and found her armour cracked in four places for her effort. She fell down on the chariot floor while infantrymen formed up around her. Guruji was not interested. He looked around and having found my battle standard, came towards it. Uttamaujas intercepted him and King Virata who had just pulled up alongside me went up in support. Guruji wounded Uttamaujas with three quick arrows, turned and in an impossible shot, took Virata's helmet clean off his head.

Guruji's focus and Kumara's death had rattled me, and I had ordered my charioteer to head back when I saw Satyaki park his chariot between me and Guruji and discharge a volley of arrows. Guruji responded by breaking his chariot axle, leaving him lying clumsily in a broken heap of wood.

Guruji's chariot slowed to approach me. I readied myself for the attack.

He was alone. The Leopard Warriors were being held back by our troops, at least for the moment.

He spoke, 'Putra, I come to talk about peace. Surrender your arms and come back to my camp and I promise you that we will make terms. I swear on my reputation as acharya of the Kuru dynasty that you will not be harmed.'

He raised his right hand to indicate his assurance when a bolt hit him hard in the ribs. Winded, he turned to look at his assailant. It was a young Yadava prince who fitted another arrow and shot him in the chest. I lifted a javelin, my last of the day, and let it fly at Guruji. Even as I let it loose, I felt guilty and was relieved to see him step out of its arc. He turned at the Yadava and fired two broad-headed arrows that crashed into his chest. The prince fell to his knees, wrapping his arms around his torso, and began coughing blood.

Guruji, still patient after going through three duels, turned back to me and said gently, 'No one else has to die. Just come with me, and you will not be hurt.' The young Yadava's coughing had stopped and I saw him fall from his chariot into the dust.

I could handle this. I was a Kshatriya. There was no reason I couldn't handle this. I just had to hold out till the reinforcements came. They would be coming any moment. I had no reason to be alarmed. I had no reason to panic. I just had to stall for time and stand my ground. I could handle this. I was trained to handle this.

I lifted up my spear and rotated it in my hands. Guruji fixed an arrow. 'Don't make me kill you, boy.'

I couldn't tell if he was bluffing. So I picked up my square shield and crouched behind it, my spear balancing on the rim of the chariot. Guruji drew an arrow and fired.

The arrow flew behind me. I turned back and saw the princes of Kekaya.

They were five, dressed in identical red armour with red dhotis trimmed in gold. I had never seen them fight individually for they always arrived as a unit, formed like an arrow head. The eldest in the front flanked by the two middle brothers, who were, in turn, flanked by the two youngest.

Guruji's arrow narrowly missed the eldest. He raised his fist and signalled his brothers to wait. Guruji regarded them, their arrows at the ready. From behind, Virata, wearing a new helmet, and Satyaki, riding a new chariot and joined by two Panchala warriors, fenced Guruji in.

Virata spoke, 'Put down your bow and move away from Yudhishthira, Drona.'

Guruji looked at the men surrounding him, and when his charioteer made to turn the horses, he tapped the man lightly on the shoulder. The charioteer put down the reins and waited.

The truth was that Virata had spoken naively. No one in that circle wanted to fight Guruji. Not even Satyaki, who had trained under him in Hastinapura and knew his tactics.

Virata spoke again, 'Drona, the bow. Put it down.' This time his voice cracked.

Guruji kept staring at me fixedly.

'Yudhishthira, come back,' Virata was losing the argument, and Guruji hadn't said a word.

My charioteer led me out of Guruji's way and took me behind Virata and the Kekayas.

'I'll count till three, Drona. Drop your bow.'

All of us had our bows drawn, praying for the old man to spare us.

'One.'

'Two.'

Guruji's charioteer snapped the reins and charged the chariot directly into us. We fired our arrows—me, Virata, Satyaki, the Panchala princes and the Kekayas. Two hit Guruji on his breastplate while the others went off their mark. I fumbled with another arrow and saw the two Kekayas on the right go down. Then the two on the left. The eldest spun out of his chariot with a dart in his collarbone. Guruji's chariot came thundering towards me with Virata, Satyaki and the Panchala princes desperately trying to intercept him.

Two arrows dislodged the left wheel of my chariot and it fell with a dull thud. I lost balance and tumbled outside. I staggered up and saw that Guruji was engaged with the two Panchala warriors along with Virata. Satyaki was a little distance behind.

The fight didn't last long. Both the Panchala warriors were killed with arrows through their necks. Satyaki took their place and fought a short duel with Guruji, matching him blow for blow, till his breastplate fell apart. Virata entered the fight and had his helmet shot off once again and bow shattered. A massive roar erupted as a group of Leopard Warriors broke through and formed a protective cordon around Guruji.

I couldn't decide whether to run or resist and waited for the last moment to arrive and push me off the cliff of my indecision.

The Leopard Warriors stalked me patiently, and I backed away, spear in hand. Clarity arrived in its tardy fashion. There was no way I could beat off so many soldiers *and* Guruji. So I really had two options—kill as many soldiers as I could before they overpowered me or not expend any strength and give up without resistance. Given a choice, I would have taken option two, thrown my spear down and walked away peacefully with them. Since I couldn't avoid capture forever, it made no sense depriving another family of its patriarch.

On the other hand, I had a reputation to maintain as a king and a war chief. I had to sacrifice myself at the altar of example for the bards to croon about for millennia.

Once again, I found myself denying everything I was, for everything I stood for.

I clenched my spear and prepared to thrust.

A cry broke out from the right but I was too preoccupied to pay attention.

A few Leopards fell in the front, arrows sticking out of their backs. A couple of them wheeled around and were cut down by darts. It was Arjuna. He was firing rapidly but his accuracy didn't appear to be affected. The Leopard Troops lost interest in me and organized themselves in a protective formation covering themselves with their shields. Guruji came up to meet Arjuna, firing bolts all the while. Arjuna dodged and shot back his own, which Guruji duly sidestepped.

Arjuna finally pierced Guruji on his chest and Guruji replied with one to his shoulder. Our boys in the infantry had begun overpowering the Leopard soldiers who were falling back. An axe-man got up from behind Guruji's chariot and tried to drag him down. Guruji smote him across the head with his bow and got hit in the ribs by Arjuna for his lapse of concentration.

Guruji's charioteer held his nerve and steered the chariot away from the fight and I saw Guruji clutch his ribs and sit down.

I dropped my spear and leaned against my chariot. For the first time that day, I began looking for my wounds. They were minor yet again and wouldn't last the night. I had lasted a whole eleven days and would fight on the twelfth.

The sky blushed purple. The day had survived us. A conch sounded, signalling the end of hostilities for the day.

I was sixteen. It was the evening before our final arms demonstration to the Kuru elders. The training pit was normally empty at this time. And I would go there to gather my wits after the day, to sit alone in the cool evening mud with a treatise on poetry. I was sitting under a torch trying to read when Guruji came out of the darkness. He looked mildly surprised to see me. I got up, dusted my back and bowed. I was not breaking any rules and was within my rights to be at the training pit till nightfall.

'Ready for tomorrow, putra?'

I nodded unconvincingly.

'Come to practise then?'

I nodded again and held the parchment tightly behind my back.

'I don't remember teaching you boys any martial art that involved wielding manuscripts.'

I looked at him sheepishly and brought the parchments.

Guruji took it and leafed through the pages.

'You're too young for this stuff.'

I raised an eyebrow.

He noticed as much and looked curiously at me.

'We're the same, you and I. You are a Brahmin in a Kshatriya's body, and I, a Kshatriya in a Brahmin's.'

He chuckled at his own observation.

His words came back to me as I saw his chariot disappearring over the shadows of Kurukshetra.

THE ELEVENTH NIGHT

RADHEYA

It had been a disappointing day, one which I wanted to end as quickly as possible. Drona was just steps away from Yudhishthira when it all went wrong. I should have gone after him myself. Drona was too slow, even with the Leopard Warriors backing him. I would have taken my pot-bellied pandit of a brother twice over and still had time to deal with Arjuna.

After hastily swabbing my bruises with a mixture of water and turmeric, I set off to the war council where Suyodhana had ordered an immediate meeting to discuss the events of the day. I didn't look at Varahamira or Shatrujeet for their opinions and went straight in.

The sabha was quiet. Shakuni stood leaning on the Speaking Staff. A wayward javelin had bruised his hip in the retreat. Shalya was also present, sitting with stiff composure. Gada warriors were used to being thrashed. He would fight tomorrow again.

'The spy reports are in. It has been confirmed. They knew of our plan to get Yudhishthira. We should have sent more soldiers after him.'

The staff went over to Bhagadatta.

'We can send every soldier we have. But the fact remains that we haven't been able to crack through their centre in the past ten days, in spite of all our Atirathis and Maharathis. My elephants have not got the support they've deserved up front.

And once we've made a start, there's been no one to follow through. Radheya, where were you today, lad? We had trimmed up the line beautifully. I thought your boys would roll them back to Indraprastha. What happened?'

He was being a little unfair now. We had gone far into the Pandava centre but Shakuni's horsemen hadn't held. Was this Drona's doing—pitting Bhagadatta against me?

I took the Speaking Staff and replied, 'I think we did well today. We pushed into the centre and cleared the way to Yudhishthira. I hear that some of the members in this council even got close enough to disable his chariot and wound him.'

Drona looked at me without flinching, 'Are you blaming me for today, boy?'

I couldn't risk an open conflict with Drona. Not yet.

'Not at all. I truly believe the day went well. Think about it, Yudhishthira was protected by Virata, Drupada, Satyaki, Shikhandi, Abhimanyu and some more whose names I don't know. That's more than Grandsire had around him.'

Drona scratched his beard absent-mindedly and was silent.

'You may be right, suta.'

I continued, 'It's good that they know of our plan to capture Yudhishthira. Saving his frightened hide will distract their attention from actually winning the fight. We should keep tomorrow's plan simple. The more soldiers we can divert away from Yudhishthira, the better will be our chances of taking him. We should attack in two forces. One to distract the Pandava effort, and one to bring Yudhishthira home.'

Shakuni nodded, 'Agreed. Radheya's right. Don't complicate anything. Simple plan. Stick to it.'

Suyodhana spoke, 'But that's what we tried today. Arjuna

still broke through our ranks and got to his brother. How do we stop that tomorrow? And if not Arjuna, there will be Bhima to contend with. And their troops. The Indraprastha Chariot Corps are the best fighting force in Kurukshetra.'

I caught Kritavarma shift in his chair. His Narayanis had never got such praise from Suyodhana.

Finally, Bhagadatta stood up.

He looked into Suyodhana's eyes and spoke, 'I see in this august gathering Atirathis, Maharathis, great warriors of every nation—Gandharas, Kiratas, Kambojas, Pisachas, Yadavas, Trigartas, Pragjyotishas and Kurus. We have nothing to fear from the Indraprastha Chariots or Arjuna or Bhima, and I shall prove it to you tomorrow. Bhima's death is on my head. Let no one come between us.'

Bhagadatta's words took some of the lines off Suyodhana's face.

He spoke softly, 'Are you sure, sire?

'Positive. I will show you children how it's done.'

Tension is a pimple; confidence, a prick. The sabha tittered like little girls.

Shakuni spoke, 'Bhima's settled then. That leaves Arjuna. Radheya?'

A deep voice interrupted me.

'Wait, please.'

We turned.

It was the king of the Trigartas, a man they called Susharma. I didn't know much about him or his five brothers who had brought a few ankinis onto the field. Their motive for entering the war was some old feud with Arjuna. Susharma was a thin, humourless man, almost completely hairless except for a thin moustache that outlined his lip. For the most part he didn't talk to anyone. If he had an opinion on the way the war was being fought, he kept it to himself.

'I want Arjuna.'

Suyodhana and I looked at each other and then at Drona, who looked tiredly at the ground when he spoke.

'And why do you think you'll be able to do a better job of killing him than the lord of Anga who, for all his defects, is still a Maharathi?'

He spoke without emotion, but everyone in the room felt his intensity.

'Arjuna plundered our lands. His men burned our cities, killed our people. We have come here not for your kingdom, but to avenge ours. We will not fail. Use our hatred.'

The sabha went silent.

Drona rubbed his eyes tiredly and nodded his approval.

Suyodhana spoke, 'Right, so we'll split forces. Lord Bhagadatta with the Trigartas will take out Bhima, Arjuna and the Indraprastha Corps. Guruji, Radheya, Kritavarma and I will go out and get Yudhishthira. The rest of you...'

While he assigned battle positions, I looked at Drona. He looked frail. Almost unwell.

Far too many combatants on either side of the war could not fight with any real hatred. I had heard from a frustrated Suyodhana that he suspected Grandsire of conveniently misfiring at the Pandavas on more than one occasion, shielded by the alibi of advancing age. I suspected Drona was a little sentimental about fighting Arjuna too. Before the war, he used to unashamedly call Arjuna his greatest pupil ever.

I sounded out Suyodhana after the council. 'What's with

Drona? He seems upset.'

Suyodhana winced. He still wasn't used to hearing his Guruji's first name referred to so casually in conversation. I didn't care. He wasn't my Guru. In fact, both Drona and I had studied under the same master, Parashurama, Rama of the Axe. A Brahmin who had taken to the arts of war after his father had been murdered on a whim by a king. Eventually, Guruji learned to wield the axe well enough to take the king's head in a duel. Even now his name was feared among the royalty, who were always looking nervously for hints of an uprising in their own kingdoms. Guruji had long since retired his killing axe and spent more time teaching young Brahmin men martial arts and self-defence. His ashram was outside the law of any kingdom, and all the kings of Bharatvarsha turned a blind eye to its activities, fearing an even greater uprising if something were to happen to him.

'No, what's wrong? He seems fine.'

'Fine? He agreed with everything that was said today.'

'Well, what's not to agree with? The plan works, right?'

'It's good. I just felt he wasn't all there today.'

'He's like that sometimes. I think the last few days have been a little rough for him.'

I nodded. No point worrying Suyodhana more than necessary. 'You're probably right. Let's see tomorrow.'

Suyodhana was silent for a moment: 'We'll capture him. Take away their kingdom and kill them all anyway. I promise, Radheya.'

That said, he fumed off in the direction of his tent.

Finally Grandsire's reason for letting me have the kingdom was clear. Neither Suyodhana nor Yudhishthira would leave each other alive if they came to the throne. I was probably the best chance for stability the Kurus had.

The thought left me cold.

A man was waiting for me outside my tent. It was Laxman, Suyodhana's son, and my favourite student. He had studied under me for the past five years on his father's insistence and had become an exceptional archer. He was only eighteen now but I was confident he would make all the kings of Bharatvarsha tremble in a few years. I would be one of them myself, I remembered, if Grandsire's plan came into effect. Suyodhana, being occupied with more pressing concerns, had entrusted the job of looking after the boy's safety to me. So I had kept him in the reserves for the past couple of days. Now he was chafing to come in front. Our conversation was brief. He told me he wanted to be in a fight, and I promised to include him nearer the killing tomorrow.

I watched him walk away, a slightly happier soul.

When I was a little younger than him, I had approached Drona's academy in Hastinapura and had been turned away with the familiar excuse—'Learn to drive a chariot, suta.'

So I had gone to Parashurama and lied to him about my background, calling myself a Brahmin and not a suta when I enrolled, and was accepted as his student. Soon I proved myself the best amongst his students and then became his favourite.

It was late in the evening that day. I was in the armoury, polishing arrowheads and returning them to their quivers. A prolonged session of yoga next to an anthill had left me with bite marks all over my legs. Though I remember the red marks dotting my thighs, it isn't the pain that I remember from that day.

He stood at the entrance to the armoury and spoke in a soft voice.

'Radheya, are you the son of a charioteer?'

I pretended I didn't know what he was talking about.

'Guruji?'

'Some of the other students claim that they have proof. I just want to know what the truth is.'

So I told him everything, including my humiliation at Drona's military academy.

When I finished, he didn't shout at me, like he did when I missed those targets on the training ground or forgot an important theorem.

'Radheya, you have lied to me. If you had come and told me yourself, I may have considered otherwise. But to enter my school, my island of trust, and stay secure in the knowledge of my ignorance?'

I hung my head.

'Leave, Radheya. And don't show your face here ever again. Before you go, I'll give you one final lesson. It will hold you good for life. Don't betray a person's trust to enter his life, or to leave it. If you forget this, everything I've ever taught you will come to naught.'

Would Laxman forgive me when I betrayed his father?

Varahamira and Shatrujeet interrupted my thoughts. They had some interesting news. A nasty rumour was spreading through the camp that the Great War was a conspiracy; that it had been started to purge humanity of all its male members leaving only a few kings to start a new master race. The real objective of this war was to wipe out the foot soldiers and low-class nobility to clear the road for the princes.

If only they knew. The Pandavas were married into the Panchalas, the Matsyas and the Yadavas. The three biggest kingdoms in Bharatvarsha were joined together in an alliance that made all the other kingdoms a little less sure of their legacy. This wasn't, as the bards still proclaimed, a war to reclaim Draupadi's honour and the Pandavas' birthright. It was the only way to protect our kingdoms from an empire that would swallow us whole.

I had a question for them before they left.

'Any news on my bounty?'

They looked at each other. Shatrujeet grinned.

'Two chests of silver and one of gold, my Lord.'

Grandsire's bounty had been four chests of gold and Arjuna's three.

Not bad for a first day.

The torches were out in camp when they left. Except in the north, where the Trigarta quarter lay.

YUDHISHTHIRA

I stood ahead of my brothers to offer our condolences for Drupada's loss.

As the eldest, I had to be the first in line to perform all the unpleasant tasks, shielding my brothers from the awkwardness such encounters inevitably yield.

Being the eldest also meant that I had to take full blame

for all the family's misfortunes. Posterity would remember me as the man who let his wife be disgraced in public. But no one would even think of blaming my siblings for not storming the sabha that day and killing Sushasana.

Drupada looked through me when I spoke and walked out of the council meeting when I had finished.

Krishna advised us to begin without him. Dhristadyumna's heart was not in it. He just sat down with his head hung. Shikhandi was in no mood to talk as well. Virata was grimacing in pain every few moments and Chekitana did not have the authority to begin a discussion. It fell on me to steer the council.

'Our information was correct. It appears the Kauravas want to take me captive.'

Virata spoke through gritted teeth, 'We were lucky today. Drona had us. If Arjuna hadn't made it, we would be making conditions for your release by now.'

Arjuna nodded in acknowledgement.

So Arjuna saves the day again. I was grateful, of course. Or at least I did a good job pretending. Inside I was throwing a tantrum. I loved Arjuna. But just once I wished I could get the chance to save his bones. Bhima, Arjuna, even Nakula and Sahadeva were more responsible for my protection than I, the head of the family, was for theirs.

Our great-grandfather was a man called Shantanu. He was the undisputed king of the Kurus, and the most powerful man in Bharatvarsha in his times.

He had three sons—Devadatta, Vichitravirya and Chitrangada.

Chitrangada died in a battle with the Gandharas and it was left to Devadatta and Vichitravirya to produce offspring and take the lineage forward.

Devadatta did not have any children. Maybe the idea itself did not appeal to him. But that didn't stop the bards from singing glowingly about him making a vow of celibacy to his father so that the rule of the land passed to Vichitravirya, Shantanu's favourite son.

Despite this there were other things to keep young Devadatta occupied. He went on a rampage, destroying armies, plundering towns and cities, bringing entire countries to their knees and expanding the Kuru kingdom to much of its present glory while Vichitravirya looked after affairs at home.

Devadatta became Bhishma, the terrible one.

And Vichitravirya married not one, but two women.

His first wife gave birth to a blind child—Dhritrashtra. His second gave birth to our father, Pandu.

Despite being younger, Pandu was considered heir to the throne and was trained in the arts of war and statecraft.

Dhritrashtra was neglected.

When Vichitravirya died, Pandu became king, and together with his Uncle Bhishma, took the Kuru empire places it had never been. Bhishma never sought the throne, being more a puppet master than a puppet. Pandu married my mother Kunti, and then took another wife, Madri, from the Madra kingdom to strengthen our alliance with them.

Then, one day, he gave it all up.

The decision surprises the entire family till today. He was on a hunt, and killed a deer somewhat brutally. The anger in its eyes as it lay there dying changed something in my father. He went straight back and informed Grandsire Bhishma of his decision to give up the throne and all his material belongings and head to the forest to meditate on the nature of the world. Naturally his wives would come with him.

All five of us were born in the forest and spent our early years there. My father was a man seeking answers, and from whatever little I can remember, he was always going on about truth and maya.

When I was around eight, Father died.

He simply collapsed one day while he was with Madri. No one knows for certain what happened, though the bards say all sorts of slanderous things. But Madri was so stricken by his death, she killed herself. This left my mother Kunti with three children of her own, and two of Madri's. She had no choice but to return to the palace. Bhishma welcomed us with open arms, and insisted that my brothers and I treat him like a grandfather as the other Kuru princes did.

In the meantime, Uncle Dhritrashtra married the queen of the Gandharas, and gave birth to a son, Suyodhana; and ran through all the noblewomen in Hastinapura producing many offspring, all of whom he loved and cared for and brought up at the royal palace. His reputation as a goat found its way into bawdy poems that claimed he was the father of a hundred offspring, which may not have been far from the truth. While I had seen many, there were apparently entire palaces filled with them in Hastinapura.

When we came onto the scene, Bhishma wanted us, more specifically me as Pandu's eldest, to be the supreme authority in Kuru lands.

That wasn't what Dhritrashtra or Suyodhana had in mind.

What followed were years of trying to undermine each other, assassination attempts, a game of dice, and finally this—a war to end all wars.

Virata interrupted my thoughts, 'Tomorrow we shall have more troops in Yudhishthira's protection...just to be sure.'

'Yudhishthira's protection'? What did he think of himself? He was the one who needed protection, the old washcloth. I was about to protest in the strongest words my education had provided me with when Krishna interrupted.

'Not that you need any added protection, Yudhishthira, but who knows? If we get a chance to single out Guruji or Radheya or Suyodhana or any of their kings, it may improve our chances. Think of yourself as a decoy, not a victim.'

The tent opened. Drupada walked in slowly to his place and sat down with great effort. He looked me in the eyes and spoke in a hard voice, 'I'd like to apologize for excusing myself from the meeting.'

Krishna spoke gently, 'No apology is required, sire. Your son fought bravely. We will all pray for his soul.'

Drupada's presence gave strength to Dhristadyumna who started, 'We began the day taking losses from the Pragjyotisha elephants. Arjuna went quite deep into the enemy's right flank before, er, Shikhandi's message reached him.'

'Message?' This was new.

'When I saw Drona in the front, I sent a courier to Arjuna to help us out in the centre with his chariots. We couldn't have fought off Drona without him.'

I marvelled at this. Arjuna was a better chariot archer than Guruji, owing to his relative youth. But to bind the day's successes to one man when thousands had perished to hold the line?

Arjuna spoke, 'The Kaurava flank was weak today. It took

Krishna no time to get across their ranks. By the way, I met Suyodhana today, brother. Left him alive for you.'

Bhima nodded wryly, 'Oh? Well, God bless you for that.'

Bhima and Arjuna shared a macabre camaraderie which I thankfully would never be a part of.

Shikhandi spoke, 'Abhimanyu acquitted himself well today. He fought Shalya, a couple of minor princes and Jayadratha.'

'Jayadratha?' This came from Arjuna, though the same question must have passed through the minds of each of us five brothers.

'Yes, the king of the Sindhus. Why?'

Bhima laughed. 'Jayadratha? I thought he'd be too scared to see us again.'

I explained to the council in less abstract terms, 'Jayadratha had tried to kidnap Draupadi when we were in exile. Unsuccessfully.'

We had met quite a few characters in our thirteen years of exile. Jayadratha was one of them. He met us at a hunting expedition close to a forest where we had set up camp. He must have seen Draupadi at the site, and started pursuing her with an earnestness that was inspired by lust. Bhima caught him trying to sneak into her quarters and we sent him back to his men gagged and tied, with the hair shaved off his head. In normal circumstances we would have just killed him and let the dogs eat his body, but princes in exile without an army cannot take such liberties.

'So he returns seeking vengeance? In any case, Abhimanyu bloodied his nose. You should be proud.'

We were. And I believe, each as proud as Arjuna, who merely nodded, avoiding any emotion in respect of Drupada's loss. In spite of the fact that we hadn't seen him grow up in Dwaraka, the boy had an exuberance that lit up any company that he kept. He was the best of the Yadavas and the Kurus, a future king of kings, a maharajadhiraj for Bharatvarsha one day.

'He is talented. That is certain. But Abhimanyu does not, um, respect the sanctity of instruction. He didn't stay in the reserves today. Shikhandi, you should have been more forceful with him,' said Dhristadyumna.

'It's all right. I let him go. No use keeping a young man out of a fight. He should be in the front.'

'The council made its decision yesterday. You could have told us then.'

'Maybe I changed my mind.'

Dhristadyumna glared at his sister. 'Maybe you should listen to your commander-in-chief.'

The entire council joined in to calm the two down.

Krishna spoke, 'My Lords, forget about all of this. The day's action is over. Let's plan for tomorrow. I agree with you, Shikhandi, we should put the boy up front. He will be valuable in the coming days, and suspending him or putting him in the back will not help our cause. But the young lout needs a little spanking. As commander-in-chief, this is far below Dhristadyumna's purview. Arjuna, please do what's needed.'

Arjuna nodded.

Clean. In a few words, Krishna had made Shikhandi look like a visionary and soothed Dhristadyumna's ego.

We spent the rest of the meeting discussing tactics.

ABHIMANYU

Father waited patiently outside my tent till my servant informed me of his presence. He didn't need to, of course, but Father wouldn't enter any man's tent without prior permission. I went out to greet him, and for the hundredth time, scolded him mildly for not treating my tent as his own.

He came straight to the point.

'Shikhandi tells me you fought well today.'

'Killed a prince or two, defeated the king of the Sindhus and rattled Uncle Shalya. Nothing great.'

'Weren't you supposed to be in the reserves?' he said softly.

Father never raised his voice to discipline me, unlike Mother. But to mend fences with him was also a great deal harder.

He continued, 'You know, in any other army, you would have been executed.'

'I'm sorry.'

'I expected more from you. It's been eleven days now. Tomorrow, you will apologize to the council. If they accept, you will fight and stay put where you're told, if you're allowed to fight at all.'

He couldn't be serious. I could do more damage to the Kauravas single-handedly than most of the council put together. They weren't actually going to send me home in the middle of the battle? I couldn't tell if he was bluffing but I didn't want to take a chance.

'I'm sorry if I offended anyone. I will apologize.'

That relieved him. He smiled awkwardly, 'So, I heard you killed a nobleman from the north today.'

'I beat the king of Sindhu too.'

'Jayadratha?'

'That's the one.'

'Shikhandi had good things to say. So did Virata.'

'That's kind of them.'

'You've just begun to create a reputation. To see it come apart, because you couldn't hold your bow in the reserves for one day, would be unfortunate. This is not an exercise for fame like the Ashvamedha. Dying will not win you glory. Surviving will give us a kingdom.'

That was all. Father kept his speeches short. Imparting wisdom embarrassed him. After looking at me awkwardly for a few moments, he went away. Typical Father, complimenting me with the words of others.

We never had a chance to get close. For most of the first eight years he was away on some war or the other and then he disappeared for thirteen years on exile.

Mother took complete control of my education. When I informed her that I wanted to take up the bow and be a warrior just like my father, she couldn't have been happier.

That is when I began practising. 'Drilling' is closer to the truth. I practised from dawn till late evening when the fireflies came out. 'Extra time in training won't kill you, and it won't get you killed either' was what Mother firmly told anyone who thought that I was spending too much time at the akhara.

It seemed I was eating every waking moment of the day. Almonds in the morning with watermelons or bananas or mangoes depending on the season; a whole roast chicken for lunch along with the staple dry wheat bread of warriors, baatis in the evening and more roast meat for dinner.

In between all this there were potions made of tulsi or neem or karela depending on what the latest craze was among the palace physicians. And there were sweets—laddoos of jaggery and barley, chunks of solid khoya and sweetened milk. Whatever the maids were able to sneak in to contribute to the cause of making the young prince grow up and become king quickly.

By the time I turned thirteen, I looked twenty.

That was the year my education truly began. I had been rudely woken up before dawn by Mother's handmaiden and summoned immediately to the royal garden. It was the middle of summer and the scent of mango and dew-wet leaves stuck to the air like it always did in the humid summers of Dwaraka.

Mother was sitting there with Uncle Krishna and a young man with a physique that most would attribute to yogis in tapasya rather than warriors. He wore a green dhoti and had a grey shawl across his shoulders.

'Ah, so the young warrior finally arrives to save the day.'

I stuck my tongue out at my uncle and was cuffed around the head by Mother.

He continued, 'Putra, we're all delighted to see the effort you're putting into your practice. And while your trainers have done competently, both your mother and I feel that perhaps you require a more, how shall I put it, professional edge to your lessons. Meet your new Guru, Pradyumna.'

The young man stood up and smiled shyly at me. 'Guru makes me feel old. Call me by my name.'

He became my mentor and more of a Guru to me than he'd care to admit.

He taught me governance, statecraft and economics through drama, poetry and literature. I learnt the twelve principles of taxation in the form of quartrains ending with vowels; the duties of a warrior in a two-act play and the four types of soil in the form of a debate between mud and manure.

More importantly, he taught me how to use the bow in a team of warriors and how to organize an attack and a defence on the battlefield and the intricacies of siegecraft.

Three years of being his shishya prepared me for the rest of my life.

THE TWELFTH DAY

YUDHISHTHIRA

Abhimanyu made a long apology to Dhristadyumna, placing the blame, as elders would to boys his age, on youth and lack of patience. The rest of us sat in our places, conscious of his desperation. Old Virata smiled, probably remembering his own reckless self ages ago.

He overdid it a little, making Dhristadyumna sound like our sole hope at Kurukshetra, calling him a peerless commander and a senapati of unrelenting vigour and brilliance who was leading us, undoubtedly, to the shores of victory. The cause would be bereft without his counsel so could he find it in his heart to forgive Abhimanyu's stupidity and excess of energy?

We heard him out patiently, and when he was done, Dhristadyumna nodded and turned to the council.

'My Lords, given, er, the circumstances we find ourselves in now, it would be unwise to suspend or remove Abhimanyu from the field. It's clear that he understands the implications of his disobedience yesterday. However, er, I still believe punishment is due.'

The rest of the council nodded. Abhimanyu lowered his head in acceptance.

'I, uh, with the council's permission, would have Abhimanyu stripped off his rank as ankini commander. He will fight as a common chariot warrior today.'

Abhimanyu relaxed and Dhristadyumna looked at him sharply, making him straighten up again.

Rank had no meaning for the boy as long as he was out there in front; so much his father's son.

'Having said that, I also feel that his talents for uncivilized conduct have been under-utilized...er, so I would have him in the front today with his father.'

The council dismissed Abhimanyu, assigning his troops to Shikhandi for the day.

Dhristadyumna spoke again, 'We've received no news of importance today. Just the regular numbers...a lot of elephants got killed yesterday. The Kauravas should be holding them back today. So, I suppose that *is* good news. I expect Radheya's chariots to be in the front. If they still mean to capture you Yudhishthira, I suppose Drona, Radheya, Suyodhana or, uh, Kritavarma and Shalya will play a role. A Chandrakala should do the job.'

Chandrakala was a crescent-shaped formation. Offense would be concentrated on the edges of the crescent while the centre would be deployed behind the rim where the front line stood. No surprises. Dhristadyumna wanted to keep me snug in the back.

'Uh, like yesterday, our focus will be on protecting Yudhishthira. Arjuna can push from the right flank. Chekitana from the left. The Panchalas, the Yadavas and Matsyas will make up the centre. Yudhishthira, er, you will be behind us. Your chariot will be personally protected by Satyajit and Vrika.'

Again, 'protect'?

Both Satyajit and Vrika were Panchala noblemen. Vishaka had told me this morning that since yesterday, the positions on my chariot flanks were being sought after by the Panchalas as it seemed the most likely place to find Guruji. There were murmurs of money being exchanged for the post, but nothing had been substantiated with evidence. The Panchalas knew how much Drupada wanted Guruji and the rewards that would follow his death at their hands.

Still, I was glad that the Panchalas would bear the brunt of Guruji's thrust.

'From, uh, my analysis, Drona prefers punching through the centre rather than hacking at the flanks. The Krauncha arrangement he put up yesterday was typical of him. I believe he will go with one of three arrangements: a needle, an eagle or the thunderbolt. Which is why, Yudhishthira, your position will be right at the back. As bait...to wear him down before he reaches you and, uh, hopefully to kill him.'

He smiled, pleased with his own logic.

Bhima's impatience ruined Dhristadyumna's appreciation of the fine arts of battle strategy.

'Sounds good. Let's go.'

We walked towards the chariot park. The elephant arsenal lay desolate next to it. Bhagadatta had made short work of them in the first six days. Our handful of mammoths were now used to cover chariot retreats rather than push ahead themselves. Without them, the Kaurava elephants had cowed down our forces and none of the allies wanted to be anywhere near Bhagadatta's beasts.

Taking down an elephant had become a long and tedious task. Long-speared infantry with their fifteen-foot-long wooden pikes poked at the elephants' eyes from a distance to stop them from charging. Behind them archers fired away at the mahout or the warrior on the back. The elephants would be bewildered at first, then furious, using their trunks to flick away soldiers like nutshells. They would thrust forward with their tusks, which were normally cased in iron, and gore any unfortunates who came in the way. One had to hope that a spear caught an elephant in the eye or under the jaw before it did too much damage.

Supritika was particularly terrifying in this regard. Nature had endowed her with oversized tusks that stuck unevenly out of her jaw like gnarled tree stumps. She was also larger than all the other elephants on the field. And white.

In times of lesser significance, Bhagadatta had told me that she was an albino calf abandoned by her herd. As a young king, he had been asked to hunt a ghost elephant laying waste to the jungle tribes of the east. In his wine-cut slur, he told me that he had wrestled her for three days and three nights, without weapon or armour. Finally, when exhaustion became a more difficult adversary, she pushed him aside and ran back into the jungle. He lay in the grass without moving until his retainers found him and took him back to camp. He slept for a week. And the day he awoke, he found the beast outside his camp, slaughtering his guards. When he approached her, she calmed and bent to her knees in submission. He took her into his stable and named her 'Supritika'.

Whether or not Bhagadatta, even in the prime of his youth, was strong enough to wrestle an elephant is a question I've never bothered asking. I've always preferred his version of the events.

What happened next is true. From early on it became evident that she was strongly attached to him.

A night after she arrived at the stables, she killed its other inhabitants. The mahouts had come that morning to find her up to her knees in elephant gore flicking blood with her trunk, like a child playing with water. Supritika's brutality had surprised the mahouts, but what really made them uneasy about the beast was the silence with which she conducted her carnage. Supritika never made a sound. Not that night in the stables, and not after. They began to call her Supritika the Silent. If she wanted something, she would nod and gesture to the mahout. She never roared or whimpered or trumpeted earnestly like the other elephants. And if the mahout did not understand, she gored him with her tusks until he did, or died, whichever came first. Bhagadatta himself was not spared her tantrums. If she didn't see him for a day, she would kill a mahout or tusk an elephant, prompting Bhagadatta's ministers to schedule an appointment with Supritika every day. She would accompany him on official visits, attracting crowds with her unusual colour, stampeding into them if they got too close or too loud, to the dismay of her mahouts, who were changed faster in Pragjyotisha than sacred threads. If the cost of keeping Supritika happy was more than the standards human decency should ever live up to, Bhagadatta didn't seem to notice. She was the toughest war elephant in Bharatvarsha.

I walked the path made familiar over the past eleven days. Vishaka was waiting for me at the chariot park with an enquiry from a nobleman regarding the whereabouts of his son (a chariot warrior charged with my protection) who hadn't come back to their tent yesterday. It was a cruel question with only one possible answer, which he didn't want to hear and I shouldn't have been asked to say. Still, I told Vishaka to tell him that a lot of warriors spent nights in quarters other than their own. They would surely meet at the battlefield today.

On the side, I also told him to have a word with the scavengers and the men who handled the carcasses. Death lived longer than a few seconds on the battlefield. After the day's carnage was complete, entire platoons of men would haul the carcasses off a few yojanas from camp, and prepare huge funeral pyres to expedite their ascension to afterlife. Unfortunately, the sheer numbers of the dead often resulted in many remaining unburned for a day or even two. I had witnessed the sight of these men, lying in a pile, limbs protruding at odd angles like grotesque human furniture. A separate heap had been kept for severed limbs or heads, to see if they could be joined with their owner on their final journey. These piles were protected from carrion birds and other scavenging animals by a platoon of masked archers. The afterlife was a thriving trade. Kusa grass and tinder wood were being sold at outrageous prices—a trend that showed no signs of stopping.

We had gotten used to death. We spent the whole day dealing with it, and the night lying close beside it. Soldiers reported visitations from spirits, mostly of warriors they had slayed. Arjuna had mentioned this in a talk he gave the younger officers before the battle. He had told them to try finishing duels as quickly as possible without observing the features of the person they killed. It will haunt you, he added quietly. It was easy for Arjuna to say this, he with the mighty bow and prodigious talent for war. But everyone who had survived thus far into the battle was stalked by someone's shade.

For me, it was a nameless boy from the second day. He was wearing a saffron dhoti and bronze armour. We had fought on the ground. He came at me swinging a sword several times too heavy for him. What made it tragic was the ridiculous simplicity of it. Even for a bumbling slasher like me. I stepped aside and tripped him. He fell down awkwardly and lay still, breathing heavily. His sword clattered away and was immediately appropriated by a foot soldier. The men around me began laughing at his clumsiness. I stood over him with my sword poised for a final cut, thanking my stars for an easy kill.

Then he took off his helmet.

A sixteen-year-old's stubble on his cheek, and a child's fear of death in his eyes. He was younger than Abhimanyu and probably as talented in combat as I had been at his age. The laughing around me stopped. The soldiers looked at me curiously, wondering what I would do next.

War. Any kind of physical conflict is mechanical by nature. An artificial momentum needs to be created and maintained to distract our mind away from the horrors we commit. Once this momentum is broken, and we become aware of ourselves, we cannot fight.

The momentum changed for both me and the boy when I saw his face. I stood over him taking in his face and his youth. The realization that I was about to kill a child stayed my hand. I stood there staring at him for what seemed like a very a long time, though it must have been only for a few moments. The silence changed tenor from curiosity to embarrassment. Strangely, the child did not move. We just looked at each other awkwardly.

I remember thinking of letting him go. I could not kill him now. Not with such coldness. I looked at the faces of my men around me stupidly, expecting one of them to resolve my moral conflict. They refused to meet my eyes and looked away.

I took a deep breath and slammed my shield into his face, hoping to disfigure it enough not to remember it later on. He fell back and found his motion, crawling back slowly, God only knows where. I lifted my sword and brought it down on his head with all my strength. His head split open like a watermelon. I pulled out my sword, trailing little grey worms that were his brain, and thick, black blood. His eyes flickered dumbly and tongue lolled and he died. I walked away. The slaughter resumed as usual.

That night, he visited me.

His head was full, but the tongue lolled, and the eyes blinked with only the whites visible. I woke in a cold sweat and couldn't sleep again that night. He didn't come after that, but I saw his face sometimes during battle. And it took all the mental discipline I possessed to run him out of my thoughts.

Perhaps death on a battlefield is better than living with yourself and a head full of ghosts.

An indistinguishable medley of voices shook my thoughts. The chariot park spread out in front of me. My brothers had reached earlier and were getting their arms in order. It was ironic, all my brothers were in front where all the carnage was, and all of Dhristadyumna's brothers were at the back with me. And yet, the day still looked more dangerous for his brothers. Sahadeva looked at me and smiled in conciliation. I had inadvertently solved the crisis of our dwindling Indraprastha Corps.

All I had to do was stand at the back and wait for Guruji.

RADHEYA

Drona had arranged us like a Garuda, an eagle with long wings and a small beak, to pierce the Pandava lines. Dhristadyumna

sought the safety of a half-moon. Yudhishthira, I guessed, would be at the back.

The eagle's beak had Drona, who was looking a lot better since yesterday, and the Leopard Guard at its tip reinforced by Suyodhana, commanding a platoon of elephants, Kritavarma and myself, supported by an elite group of Yadava and Anga chariots. The beak would detach from the main force once we got close enough to Yudhishthira.

The rest of our bird stretched out behind us across the field,
Directly behind us were Bhagadatta's Pragjyotisha elephants and hidden from view were the Trigartas behind them.

The right wing was led by Shalya, looking almost normal now. The left wing was in the hands of Drona's son, Ashwatthama, an easily dislikeable character prone to fits of violent rage. The reserve would be in Jayadratha's charge today.

The bird bristled as the battle conches began their first blare. Kurus, Kambojas, Yavanas, Daradas, Kalikeyas, Sakas, Abhiras, Kalingas, Surasenas, Madras, Amvashthas, Magadhas, Paundras, Madrakas, Gandharas, Sakunas, Vasatis—we had members from almost every civilized kingdom. The stone-like mountain men from the north—grey-complexioned; uncomplaining and ever silent slit-eyed head hunters from the far east; green- and blue-eyed foreigners from across the seas with strange symbols tattooed on their arms and unpronounceable names.

It was not impossible that the entire world was represented here on these plains. Men from the pits of the earth to its very lofts stood here on this ground in Bharatvarsha. Men of all kinds talking in every possible tongue we could imagine, telling stories of their ways, their women, home, and their desire to return and never leave.

The Pandava conches responded, louder it seemed, making contest of this too. I could make out Arjuna with Bhima and Abhimanyu. That was good news. Bhagadatta and the Trigartas wouldn't have to wander around the battlefield locating their targets.

A second round of conches blasted from our lines, outdoing the Pandava effort. A few seconds later the Pandavas returned their call with the same ferocity. The battle would begin on the third blast. I gripped my bow tightly.

It didn't sound.

Puzzled, I looked at Suyodhana and Kritavarma, who shrugged and asked the soldier next to him to find out about the delay. Drona didn't turn around and looked on calmly at the battlefield. There was a rustle of motion from behind us, and Susharma walked out of the lines.

I called out to him, but he paid no attention. Kritavarma shouted out too, but Susharma kept walking. Drona continued looking impassively towards the battlefield.

He was unarmed and wore a white dhoti and cuirass. Curiously enough, he appeared to have and had shaved off his eyebrows and moustache. He walked at an easy pace towards the centre of the battlefield, where the two armies would meet. A hundred bows rose up on either side. A few paces away from the Pandava centre, he stopped and began to speak.

We couldn't hear him, but everyone was already forming their own theories. Was Susharma backing out? Was he defecting to the Pandavas? Our entire army went silent trying to make out his words when Drona turned around and said loudly to the army in general:

'It's all right. It's part of the plan.'

What plan?

I was furious. The old rat hadn't discussed any plan in the council yesterday. Susharma and his Trigartas were supposed to find Arjuna and kill him over the course of the battle. By the looks of it, Susharma was challenging Arjuna directly. So now the Pandavas knew that we were targetting Arjuna as well. It appeared Drona had no faith in the element of surprise.

A murmur went up from behind. I looked. The Trigartas made their way to the front of the line ahead of Bhagadatta and my heart nearly stopped. Ten thousand soldiers, at least two thousand chariots. Dressed in white dhotis, armours painted hastily overnight in a dull, patchy white. Their eyebrows and the hair on their faces had been shaved off.

It would have been easier to paint a bull's eye on them. In front of us stood more than ten thousand soldiers, handpicked to be killed by Arjuna, coloured for his convenience.

Susharma walked back to the lines with grim pride. He took his position at the head of the Trigartas and nodded at Drona, avoiding eye contact with any of us.

Someone tapped me on the shoulder. I looked back to find Kritavarma looking annoyed.

'So it appears Guruji told Susharma to make a public act of it.'

'Why didn't he ask the council?'

Kritavarma shrugged.

'That's not all, you know.' He nodded towards the white soldiers who looked like caricature ghosts. 'They're calling themselves Samsaptakas now.'

I blinked.

Samsaptakas—warriors bound by oath to slay an enemy

or die on the battlefield. It meant that they could not return from the field until their target had been killed. If they were unsuccessful, they would kill themselves when the war was over.

Kritavarma continued, 'Seems yesterday night they made funeral arrangements...bought firewood and kusa grass and wrote their final letters. Their couriers have been sent off with explicit instructions not to return. Their retainers and camp followers have also been paid in full and told to leave as soon as their master falls.'

Susharma had always seemed an intense man, and I had felt that yesterday's act was more bravado to fire up the council than serve any practical purpose. Apparently not. Susharma was taking his role of Arjuna slayer very seriously. And he had doomed himself and his men on the way.

The conches sounded again. The Trigartas, or Samsaptakas now, charged ahead of our front line causing confusion in our ranks. In the distance I could make out Arjuna break off from the main force with a small contingent to meet them. As the Samsaptakas streamed out, I looked at Drona, whose expression was still blank. He looked at me and Kritavarma and then spoke to his charioteer. His chariot clattered noisily and thundered down the field at a charge. I should have left the old bastard to die. Instead, I nodded at Narasimha and followed Drona, trying to catch up. My Anga chariots started behind me in haste but managed to get in each other's way and stopped.

Kritavarma rode parallel to me with his Yadava chariots behind him in a perfect line, not one hoof out of place.

I didn't expect any less of them. They were Narayanis, after all—guardians of Dwaraka, perhaps the best individual fighting unit in the known world. They were picked from the best soldiers in the Yadava confederacy and personally trained for five harsh years. They wore yellow dhotis with dark blue armour and their breastplates were embossed with a plough, symbolic of their mastery over any kind of weaponry. It was rumoured the Narayanis could make a lethal weapon of straw and dust.

I looked back at my own ragged line of Anga chariots, now reassembling slowly, and sighed. Narasimha was good at the hacking and maiming parts of war, but he was no organizer of lines or keeper of discipline.

Drona's chariot went full tilt into the Pandava lines. His Leopard Guard, on chariots today, shored up behind him. Together, they punched clean into the Pandava front with little resistance. I held back for the Narayanis and my own Angas to come, but it didn't look like Drona needed our help.

His bow rose, changed direction and fired without a jerk in the motion. His awareness of the enemy was sublime. He swivelled from left to right, knowing exactly who was close enough to hit. And every arrow hit a target. Mostly on the head or in the face. After a few moments of confusion, the Pandava soldiers became aware of his intentions and a small circle cleared up around him as he pushed forward, looking for Yudhishthira. He was oblivious to his surroundings now, firing away mechanically, using his immense concentration to find his target.

I was reminded of a story I had heard about the Pandavas when they were children. Drona had given them an archery test. He had hidden a wooden parrot in the branches of a tree thick with foliage and asked them to aim for its eye. Before they took their shot, he asked them what they saw to which

all of them said that they could see the parrot. Wrong answer.
Drona didn't let them take the shot. When Arjuna came up to
take aim, he told Drona that he could see just the parrot's eye
and nothing else. This pleased the old man immensely. He had
told them proudly that *that* was the kind of focus one needed
to maintain on the battlefield.

Drona went deeper into the Pandava army supported by the
Leopard Guard. Kritavarma and I came up behind them followed
by our brigades, almost entirely untouched. Something was not
right. We were pressing into the Pandavas far too quickly. The
Pandava soldiers stood around us, making half-hearted attempts
at attacking us and withdrawing just as suddenly.

It was too easy.

A trap.

As it struck me, I looked around for Kritavarma and
desperately motioned my chariot towards him. A great
commotion rose in the back. The Pandava infantry had come up
from behind us, cutting us off from our main army, swallowing
the eagle's beak in their centre. Their foot soldiers now joined
shields and marched slowly towards our chariots. In our hurry
to pick out Yudhishthira, our chariots had left the infantry
behind and now we were defenceless against their long spears.
I looked around. Suyodhana and his elephants were fighting
their way towards us, but they wouldn't reach us in time.
Kritavarma and the Narayanis were assembling in the midst
of the confusion with serene calm while the Leopard Guards
were taking great pains to shield Drona who was still looking
blindly for Yudhishthira.

I had gotten separated from my Anga contingent so I joined
Kritavarma and his Narayanis. He was at the centre of his troops,

directing action, when I reached him. 'It's a trap. We'll have to fight our way out.'

He replied without looking at me, 'Without the old man?'

I saw Drona make his way still further into the Pandava army. Most of the Leopard Guard had been cut to pieces behind him. He was almost completely isolated but didn't seem to care. A lost cause, if ever there was one.

'We can't help him. Let's just go.'

Kritavarma was silent.

'Have you seen him? He's gone mad. He's not going to listen to us,' I hissed.

He looked uncertain. 'I'm not sure.'

'We don't have time, Kritavarma!'

He nodded and barked a short order. The Narayanis came together beautifully. A wedge was formed fluidly in moments.

The only problem was it pointed in the wrong direction.

Towards Drona.

I looked at Kritavarma, who sounded the charge. It would be useless to break out in the opposite direction alone, so I loaded an arrow and told my chariot to move with the Narayanis. Kritavarma saw me keeping pace with his troops and smiled.

'Good. I hoped you would see things my way.'

I smiled back at him. Smarmy bastard, I would wrap that tongue around his face one day.

We pushed through the Pandava spears at full tilt, crushing dust and bones in our wake, and made for Drona who was still going strong.

The Panchala infantry blocked our path, a few feet away from him.

I was amazed that the Pandavas didn't just attack him

from the back and end his life. It seemed that they were taking elaborate measures to keep him alive and I soon learned why.

Dhristadyumna came into view on his chariot and called out Drona for a duel.

So, the Pandava strategy was directed by Panchala revenge.

The Panchalas surrounded Drona and goaded him towards Dhristadyumna while we fought hard to reach him.

I was tired. My arms ached as I shot arrows into a never-ending mass of Pandava soldiers. The veins erupted through my arms as I pulled relentlessly. The strain was beginning to tell on the Narayanis too. A chariot warrior next to me kneeled on the floor of his chariot, desperately trying to free the cramps in his fingers, and was caught by a Pandava arrow. Slowly, the Pandava troops began pushing us further from Drona.

He was facing Dhristadyumna now, surrounded by Panchala foot soldiers. It was apparent that they had been given specific instructions by Dhristadyumna not to harm him. I heard him clear through the sound of battle. 'Satanika, Ketama, Panchalya, Now!'

The three of them surrounded Drona. All of them looked grim.

I was betting on Drona.

My neck snapped back, jarring my vision for a moment. An arrow had hit my helmet, scraping my scalp. I sat down in the chariot and removed my helmet. The Narayanis on my flank, God bless them, protected me while I regained the use of my head. A few moments of rest and I stood up again.

One of Drona's opponents lay on the ground without a head, his neck oozing blood. Another was slumped over the side of his chariot. The third was in the dust with a clump of arrows in his chest. The only one standing was Dhristadyumna, though just barely. Arrows were stuck in both his arms, which he was trying to remove with great patience.

An arrow smashed into his chest and he stumbled back. The Panchala soldiers stood around horror-struck. They had obviously received instructions not to interfere and were debating the same. I looked at Drona. He stood with a couple of arrows stuck loosely on his breastplate, but otherwise unhurt.

Dhristadyumna picked up a bow and made a pathetic attempt of mounting an arrow. Drona let him load his arrow, and then, with careful aim, shot at his arm again. The arrow missed. But it was enough to set off the Panchalas, who howled and crowded around Drona's chariot while another lot pulled Dhristadyumna away.

At that moment, Kritavarma saved Drona.

He sounded a charge and we broke through the Panchala troops separating us from Drona and took positions around him.

I stretched my fingers around the bow handle. Two of the three quivers of fifty arrows I carried were empty. I must have killed at least thirty soldiers and it wasn't even afternoon. The Narayanis, what was left of them, some sixty-odd, formed a circle with Drona in the centre. I joined him and Kritavarma as the Panchalas began closing in.

Drona looked at me and grinned, 'This is what we call a battle, suta.' Dust outlined the creases in his face but his eyes were those of a man much younger. Stupid old fool, running us into a trap.

I was too tired to respond. I leaned on my bow as the Narayanis began falling around us.

Kritavarma looked at me, 'Done so soon? We have to take

at least a couple of hundred with us, you know?'

I picked up my bow, heaved an arrow out of its quiver and took a chariot archer in the eye.

There were very few Narayanis left now and the three of us. We moved in closer together as the Panchalas picked off the Narayanis one by one. They were leaving us for the end. We killed as many soldiers as we could. It would soon be our time.

A trumpet sounded to our west.

The Panchalas began to scatter as a horde of elephants trampled their way towards us. Suyodhana was at their head and moments later we were surrounded by friendly faces. Anga troops among them. I spotted Narasimha. His face was a bloody mess and his mood was surly as ever. A good sign.

'You're finding new ways to look ugly, Simha.'

He grimaced, 'Spear caught the cheek. Wish someone would tell the bastards to use 'em only on elephants and not men.'

I would take his arse in the evening for not being able to put our troops in a straight line. But now I just told him to get everyone together and follow me.

Kritavarma pulled up next to me. 'No Narayanis left here. I'll be riding with you.'

'My pleasure. Seen the old man?'

'Up front with the tusks. I think he's found Yudhishthira. Not sure though.'

We found Drona among the elephants in a tiny chariot. Kritavarma and I worked our way carefully up to him, staying as far away from the elephants' feet as we could.

He beamed at us as we approached, 'Yudhishthira's right in front. We should have him in no time.'

I peered through dust and elephant limbs. Yudhishthira was

on a chariot aiming a javelin surrounded by a small troop of chariots.

Drona signalled to Suyodhana who was directing the elephants' progress and took his chariot ahead towards Yudhishthira. Kritavarma looked at me and shrugged and followed him. The two of them rushed towards the Pandava chariots. I sighed and told my charioteer to follow. I was going to be a victim of Drona's recklessness twice in the same day.

YUDHISHTHIRA

The elephants had materialized as if from dust.

One moment our men were decimating the Narayanis, the next, their blood was warming elephant feet. Guruji, Radheya and Kritavarma were one simple order away from being killed. Then Dhristadyumna's Panchala-sized ego thought of asserting itself. Did he really think that he, Satanika, Ketama and Panchalya were going to pose a serious threat to Guruji's time on earth?

I saw it from a distance. Three of them were dead in the time it took to lift their arrows out of the quivers. Dhristadyumna had his armour smashed and arms run through with arrows. If the Panchala foot soldiers hadn't pulled him off his chariot, we would have had to hunt the battlefield for pieces of him to cremate. For a moment, I was relieved that Drona was only supposed to capture me, and did not seriously want me dead. A sensation that was quickly replaced by shame.

The elephants came then. And I watched our chances of winning the war that afternoon disappear under their feet. Three of the most important generals of the Kaurava army, who were almost in our hands, were all rescued unharmed. Just because Dhristadyumna wanted a Panchala end for Guruji.

And now Guruji was separated from me only by a few chariots. He was flanked by elephants and had Kritavarma at his side and Radheya at his back.

It was becoming a little desperate. My palms had begun sweating. My javelin stuck to the sea of dew that was my palm. My lips were dry, and my other hand went across the cabinet on my chariot in search of my water pouch while my eyes stood fixed at Drona's progress.

Satyaki and Shikhandi, supported by Uttamaujas and Yudhamanyu, moved to cut him off. Good, I had more faith in the two of them than Dhristadyumna and his band of Panchala goons.

They formed a diamond and approached Guruji cautiously. While they occupied him, I sent a horseman to call in the reserve. Even Guruji wouldn't be able to wade through ankinis of fresh soldiers.

To my horror, Kritavarma and Radheya came in front of Guruji and blocked them even as Guruji dodged away from the fight and came towards me increasing his speed.

The neatness of the manoeuvre paralysed me. I didn't notice the javelin fall out of my fingers and clatter to the floor. Satyajit and Vrika, my protectors, moved to intercept him and were both shot down immediately—Satyajit with an arrow in the neck and Vrika with one that ran through his eye and tore through the back of his helmet.

In the distance, I could see Satyaki and Shikhandi trying to break away from Kritavarma and Radheya. They would not be able to come to me in time. I had to hold off Guruji till the reserve came. I slung a quiver around my shoulder and groped around the floor of the chariot for my bow.

I looked up to see Guruji standing in front of me with his bow arched.

'It's over, son.'

I stood there stupidly holding a bow in my hand. I didn't know how to react. Attacking him would be suicide, but he was supposed to take me alive. He wouldn't shoot me. Not fatally. I began to raise my bow.

'Don't think I won't kill you if you lift that bow.'

So attacking him was clearly not an alternative. I looked around for Satyaki, Shikhandi, anyone. But the field around me was thick with Kaurava chariots. My mind was clouded and the blood was dancing in my head.

'Guruji?'

'Stop wasting time and get in my chariot.'

'My brothers won't stop fighting without me, you know.'

'No one else will die, I promise. All you have to do is come with me.'

I put my bow down and took off the quiver from my back and stepped down from my chariot.

I was about to do the one thing that he had never taught us at the training pit.

Surrender.

ABHIMANYU

The man was bald and dressed entirely in white. He looked more like a monk seeking food than a man with a kingdom. He walked slowly to the centre of the neutral ground between the armies and spoke quietly in chaste Sanskrit.

'My name is Susharma. I am the king of the Trigarta people. We have sworn on blood and holy fire that Arjuna, prince of the Pandavas, destroyer of the cities of Trigartadesa, will not see the end of the war. Make preparations for his passing as we have done for ours.'

Every person in hearing distance looked around for my father, straining to get a better view if his chariot was out of sight. Whispers skittered across the ranks like spiders.

I saw him look gravely at Susharma and nod his head. I could tell he was conscious of the gaze of the army and uncomfortable with the attention.

The silence was broken by the bass drone of my Uncle Bhima.

He comes in white,
this harbinger of fright,
without a hair on his head.
Arjuna, he'll kill,
his blood he will spill
in his dreams, while lying in bed.

Laughter crackled through the ranks. Susharma didn't react. He turned around and walked back unhurried. When he reached, an entire contingent of chariots and infantry clad just like him in white came to the Kaurava front and positioned themselves in line with where Father stood.

Father commanded the right flank of the formation and I wanted to bring my chariot closer to his, but he would not have approved. So I stood there, a few chariots to his left, hoping that Sumitra could manoeuvre a place in the front line beside him when we began to charge.

The battle conches sounded for the first time. I looked around. Uncles Nakula and Sahadeva were to my left and Uncle Bhima was to my right. The twins were talking among themselves as they always did before battle. Uncle Bhima was pointing at the Kaurava formation and making observations to his charioteer. I looked behind him for his son and waved at him. He waved back and smiled with his teeth.

We called him Ghatotkacha. If he had a real name, it was known only to his mother, the queen of a large jungle tribe in the eastern provinces who besotted Uncle Bhima during his travels. Not that he needed much provocation. The happy result was my cousin. When he was born, my uncle had jokingly called him 'Ghatotkacha' owing to the fact that his head was round like a pot and the colour of baked clay. The name stuck, and Ghatotkacha maintained his dome proudly. He looked identical to his father except he was bald and a deeper shade of brown verging on black. He had brought with him an ankini of tribal infantry who were ingenious fighters. They didn't wear armour, seeking protection in the feathers of birds and trinkets blessed by their local priest. On the battlefield, they relied on speed and acrobatics and carried short flat clubs and poison-tipped stabbing spears.

Their nakedness and rudimentary weapons marked them out in the early days of the battle where many of the enemy had gone after them foreseeing an easy kill. Not many had returned in triumph. Inspite of all this, the most peculiar thing about the tribals was not the way they fought.

They sang.

A lay of their tribe. They sang in words none but their own understood. An upbeat melody which the entire troop belted out with gusto, miraculously enough, in tune. They sang while advancing towards the enemy. They sang while killing them and by some accounts, choked out the words while the spirit escaped their own body too.

The rest of the army would cluster around their rustic tent enclosures at night to see if reckless courage could indeed be fed to an individual. The tribals had even caught the fancy of my Uncle Bhima who was threatening to teach them a line or two in Sanskrit from his own compositions.

They were warming up now, by the sound of it...humming with closed mouths in preparation. Ghatotkacha was checking the timbre of his voice too. It was an unusual way to divert one's mind before battle, but was effective, nonetheless.

The battle conches sounded for the first time and the entire army stiffened uneasily. I looked at the Kaurava formation. A Garuda, just as Dhristadyumna had predicted. He was all charts and logic, our commander. Pompous fart, crying to the council because I refused his rubbish order. I would return the favour soon.

The Kaurava front looked impressive. Guru Drona, Radheya, Suyodhana and Bhagadatta. Behind I could even make out old Shalya, looking even more like a dry stick after Uncle Bhima's pounding. It was a miracle he could stand, much less hold a spear on a chariot. Maybe Uncle Bhima had gone soft on him. Earlier on, so the rumour went, even Grandsire had looked reluctant to kill my father or any of my uncles; instead, expending his talent on kings he had never gotten along with. In hindsight, being brought up in Dwaraka, away from my cousins and Kaurava uncles, made killing them a little easier for me. I still felt a pang at times while fighting the Narayanis, many of whom I had even recognized as I released their souls with my arrows.

The battle conches sounded again and then for the third time, signalling the armies to advance. The Kaurava Garuda shambled towards us. A sharp, tapered front with the rest of the army spread out behind it, looking like a python that has just swallowed a very large animal.

The Trigartas broke off from the main army. Their king came out in front of them and roared, 'Trigartadesa, Samsaptaka!'

Their chariots started at a leisurely pace while the infantry rushed, arms at the ready, almost causing a stampede in their frenzy to get to us. Strange tactics...normally, chariots made a breakthrough and infantry followed up.

We readied ourselves for the impact. Our infantry had their shields ready and spears raised. In the chariots, we had our bows arched. Behind us, lines of bowmen awaited the command to fire protected by infantry carrying short-range weapons like maces, axes, swords and stabbing spears.

Father's voice was heard over the trembling earth.

'Archers, let them come. On my call.'

Uncle Bhima was less subtle, 'I'll kill the bastard who shoots before his time.'

The front line laughed nervously. The tension dissipated for a moment before springing back into our limbs.

Father spoke again, now a little louder, 'Archers. On the

count of three. One...two...'

A couple of arrows flew into the path of the Trigartas, harmlessly sticking into the earth before them. Father ignored the error and waited for his moment. Uncle Bhima glared behind and bellowed, 'Three, not two, you illiterate fools!'

Father's hand came up. And he swung it down sharply, raising his voice for the first time that day. 'Three ...Fire.'

Our arrows made a bridge in the sky as they arced towards the Trigarta soldiers. A good number of them were hit, some killed instantly. But they kept charging.

Something was different.

It was almost as if they were possessed. I saw one soldier with a dismembered arm, blood sluicing out of the stump, holding a shield in his good arm, running with a loud cry into our front. Many of them kept running after being hit by three or four arrows. It was like they didn't care. Like they were making a conscious effort to get themselves killed.

The Trigartas washed into our line like the ocean's froth on a beach and pushed back our front line immediately.

I was halfway through my first quiver already. The infantry around me was pushing back furiously. The chariots around me were being swept by waves of Trigartas. I saw a chariot archer dragged out of his chariot by the one-handed warrior who used his shield to crush the archer's face.

They were slowly clustering around my chariot now. Our soldiers were stubbornly holding their own, but the sheer force of the Trigarta rush was overwhelming them.

I put an arrow through a soldier who tried clambering onto my chariot and another into a mace fighter who was closing in on Sumitra. As more soldiers surrounded us, the bow was fast losing its effectiveness. This would have to be done the old-fashioned way.

I pulled out an axe from the armoury and stepped off my chariot. A swordsman slashed wildly at me. I blocked the strike with my axe and plunged its handle into his gut. The blow winded him, giving me enough time to raise my weapon and split his face in two. Bits of skin and skull and hot blood sprayed on my face. I tasted the bitter saltiness of his life streaming out as he slunk to the ground like a snake in a trance. The kill rejuvenated me and I swaggered foolishly out of my chariot's vicinity, straight into the arc of a mace.

The blow cracked my breastplate. I felt my ribs bend and fell down heavily, blinded. I blinked and the world wheezed back around me. A silhouette raised the mace to swing it down heavily on my face, I coughed and tried to rally my limbs into motion.

And then, his head fell off.

A pair of hands pulled me up. The world spun and then came to a sharp halt in front of my eyes. I coughed and retched. Blood mixed with sputum coloured the ground. I blinked and watched my spit writhe in the dust. A hand came into view and thrust a pouch of water into my face. My mouth found the sipper and I sucked slowly. Now a pair of hands guided me towards the back of a chariot and made me sit. The battlefield came together like pieces of a puzzle.

I looked up and saw Bali grinning at me. His hands spoke in their slow, calm sweeps.

'Time to get up, prince.'

I nodded.

I stumbled into my chariot and he returned to his. In the

past few moments, our forces had been able to counter the Trigartas. I heard an incomprehensible chanting from the back that grew louder.

Ghatotkacha and his heathens jogged into the Trigarta swarm with their spears at the ready and were swallowed almost instantly. Their chanting was still heard, less emphatically, over the twang of metal.

I took out my sword and a round shield and ran into the fray ignoring the frantic calls of my charioteer.

A spear lunged in my direction, which I avoided; I then cut its shaft. I rammed my shield into a face and cut another open. Someone jumped on my back and I whirled around to get him off. Another tried to run me through with his sword, which I stepped away from. The man on my back tried to wrap his arm around my neck to choke me. I bit into it. The hair tickled my tongue roughly; I released my bite to take a bigger mouthful of his hand and swung wildly. He catapulted off me and a bit of his skin tore of his hand into my mouth. I spat out his skin and walked over to him as he tried to stand and plunged my sword deep into his neck and sliced his jugular.

I stood over his carcass, trying to find my breath when something sharp pierced me in the back. A second shiver of pain ran through my shoulder. I turned and saw an archer on a stationary chariot draw his bow. He fired and missed his third shot.

My turn.

I sprinted towards him. His chariot started moving away from me. I threw my shield like a discus and it struck him hard on the shin. As he bent over, I took two giant steps onto the platform of his moving chariot and speared him through with my sword. His driver tried to escape, but I caught him by the back of his neck and yanking him back, slit his neck slowly while he struggled.

More Trigartas came up from behind. A platoon of fifteen odd approached me in a crescent, cautiously. That pleased me.

I stepped off and prepared to meet them in the traditional style, with my sword parallel to the ground and the palm of my left hand open. They circled around me, cordoning me off. There was none of the mindless fury of the beginning of the day, just a cold practicality guarding their motions as they stalked me.

I swiped tentatively at a mace fighter on my left who backed away. From my right, a sword cut at me. I dodged and took a step back, almost into a spear a man was holding behind me. I turned around to face him. He rolled his spear in his hand and shoved it at my shoulder. I bent and thrust my sword towards his groin. He backed away like a crab and warily lowered his stance. I stood my position and waited for the next attack.

A plume of dust blew through our little circle. I looked up and saw Father in his white chariot flexing his bow.

I cried out for him to stop, 'No, wait!'

It was too late. In moments, his arrows cut down half the cordon that surrounded me. I turned around and saw the rest of the cordon lying prone with arrows probing their bodies. A group of chariots followed him past me into the Trigartas behind me, scattering them away like flowers. I watched, increasingly annoyed with his success.

Sumitra came up from behind me in my chariot.

'There you are, master. Just look at your father!'
I glared at him and he fell silent.
'Follow him. No, overtake him.'

YUDHISHTHIRA

I had taken only two steps towards Guruji when the earth began to shiver under my feet.

Eight chariots skidded into our midst.

Bhima, Satyaki, Nakula, Drupada, old Virata, Shikhandi, Yudhamanyu and Uttamaujas. They faced Guruji in a neat line. Foot soldiers ran past me and filled in the gaps between them.

I quietly got back on the chariot hoping no one had seen me, and told my charioteer to join the eight. I pulled up beside them, in the extreme right corner and waited for events to unfold.

For a few moments, a tense silence filled the air between them. Bhima reached for an arrow in his quiver and Guruji fired at him before he could pick one out. Bhima ducked and swayed, and almost instantly, seven arrows flew at Guruji. Two struck him in the chest and he stumbled back.

My voice was stuck in my throat. It didn't seem right for Guruji to be killed, no, hunted down like this, like an animal in the wilderness, instead of perishing honourably in single combat. But nine against one was probably the best chance we'd ever have with Guruji.

I was too busy watching the spectacle to remember to lift my bow. But every one of the eight had their bows stretched, waiting for a clean shot. Guruji tottered on his chariot and supported himself by holding its sides. The arrows had hit deep. He would be bleeding inside the armour.

And then, a volley of arrows came from behind him.

A line of elephants charged past him, trampling towards us. We abandoned Guruji and scattered while they formed a cordon around him.

I caught up with Bhima a little ahead. He wheeled around back towards the enemy and Nakula, Shikhandi and the rest of them clustered around us.

'Aren't you supposed to be up front?'

I don't know why I said that. In a day full of cock-ups, this seemed the oddest one of all.

Bhima looked at me with an impossible combination of pity, disgust and scorn, and replied like it was the most obvious deduction in the world, 'I was called back.'

I nodded.

'What about Arjuna?'

'Still in front. Fighting Trigartas. Giving them hell.'

Bhima turned his attention to the rest of the chariots.

'Right, form an arrowhead and let's get these bastards. I'm the tip.'

The rest of us obeyed dutifully, unmindful of his relative lack of seniority compared to Virata, or in fact, me.

Bhima placed his chariot in front, and the rest of us formed behind him. Satyaki, Nakula, Virata and I formed one wing and Drupada, Shikhandi, and the Panchala princes became the other. We approached the Kauravas, who had returned to a formation with Drona in the centre flanked by Radheya and his Anga chariots on the left and Suyodhana and his elephants on the right.

Suyodhana saw me, and was about to sound a charge when a lucky javelin caught his mahout in the chest. Suyodhana jumped out of his seat and took the place of the unfortunate mahout and tried to steady the rudderless elephant. I lifted a javelin and took careful aim. I could kill Suyodhana if I threw it straight. That would end the war, perhaps? Or was that too much to ask? Bhima had sworn to kill all of Dhritrashtra's sons, but he wouldn't mind, as long as Suyodhana's killer stayed within the family.

This was *my* moment. This would be the story that would be sung about me by bards for the next hundred generations.

My hand trembled a little and I clenched the javelin tighter. It had an iron head with an extended tip reinforced with bronze. With the right amount of force, it could cut through a tree. I had only a few of these, and used them cautiously, often retrieving them after a kill.

Suyodhana was still struggling with his elephant. His legs were around the beast's neck and he was massaging the top of its head vigorously. I closed my left eye, took the Lord's name, and let the javelin fly. It arced beautifully straightening out exactly as I had seen it in my mind. It dived into Suyodhana with all the strength of my arm, and the hate of my family behind it.

My moment.

The stupid beast reared and the javelin crashed straight through its eye.

I cursed my bad luck and nearly swore. Everything was perfect about that throw except my karma.

The beast bellowed and swung its head violently, trying to dislodge the javelin. It tottered as if drunk and turned on the Kauravas, thundering through their ranks, shrieking. Suyodhana barrelled to the side and nearly fell off, but caught the beast's helmet strap and held on grimly for dear life.

I prayed that he fall and would be caught under the beast, and I would be able to claim the kill, but somehow he climbed back on top even as the beast shook its head and trampled around like a sulking child. An infantry troop of long spearmen surrounded it and jabbed at it. The beast stopped as the sharp bronze tips pinched its flesh.

It backed away a few steps and roared at them, then picked up a nearby chariot that was lying abandoned in the vicinity and used it like a broom to sweep away its attackers.

I looked at Bhima whose mouth was open as wide as his eyes. Guruji and Radheya were shouting instructions to Suyodhana, even as the elephant's manic howls drowned their voices.

I saw Suyodhana bring out a chisel-blade and hammer from the mahout seat. Standard equipment kept by all mahouts in case they lost control of their elephants. He fixed the chisel's point above the elephant's neck at the base of its spine where he sat and rammed it down hard with the hammer. The elephant's neck twisted and the beast lumbered and crashed into the earth. It writhed on the ground for a few moments even as the soldiers closed in and hacked it with their axes and spears. It mewled piteously as its spirit left its mangled frame.

Suyodhana stood perched on the ruins of the elephant and raised the hammer in his hand. A ragged cheer broke from the Kauravas.

'Before they form. Now,' I heard Bhima shout.

Before I had time to grip a spear and point it in the right direction, my chariot was already charging into the Kaurava ranks, a few steps behind Bhima, who was already swinging his mace into unsuspecting Kauravas. For a change, he had chosen to fight from the chariot. I followed him, picking off a soldier with a well-aimed javelin, and then nearly got my head caved in by an arrow.

I looked in the direction of the missile and was surprised to see Suyodhana. That he would attack me, try to maim me in his effort to take me alive was not in doubt. But with a bow? As an archer he only ranked marginally lower than one person in the whole of Kurukshetra.

I turned around to see the person in question slinging a quiver around his neck and bending his bow to make it supple.

Bhima.

Suyodhana fired at me again. He had aimed the shot at my chest but succeeded in sending it straight over my head. I lifted a javelin to heave towards him. Bhima's chariot raced across my path and he grunted 'Mine!' Simultaneously, another arrow flew past me and sank into a fallen chariot a few hundred steps away.

Bhima drew his bowstring and snapped an arrow wide off Suyodhana, who countered with an arrow that flew a good distance above Bhima's chariot. Bhima responded and nearly grazed Suyodhana's chariot wheel.

Satyaki and Nakula caught up with me, followed by reinforcements, and we started firing into the disoriented Kauravas who began to retreat.

Suyodhana and Bhima hadn't been able to hit each other. Two Maharathis using their bows like untrained novices. Every arrow flew unerringly wide, damaging nothing but bloody soil and battlefield debris.

I was about to enter the fray and end Suyodhana's life myself when an arrow that was probably aimed at Suyodhana's head flew high and cut his battle standard. The flag tumbled down and draped around one of his black horses that neighed with fright. Emboldened, Bhima fired another one. This time, the arrow smashed Suyodhana's bow clean out of his hand.

I don't know who was more surprised, Suyodhana, who stared at his bow lying in the dust broken in two pieces, or Bhima, who stared at his own disbelievingly. To cut a bow without injuring the bowman is considered a great feat for an archer. Bhima had just joined the ranks of Grandsire, Arjuna, Guru Drona and Parashurama.

I would never hear the end of it.

Bhima aimed another one. He pulled back the string with a flourish and let it go. To his credit, Suyodhana stood still in his chariot and looked at Bhima without flinching, as he waited for the arrow to hit him, which it never did. The arrow soared high above Suyodhana and was lost.

Suyodhana laughed at Bhima's effort and shouted over the distance between them, 'If your wife could see you now, she'd switch sides! When you write her tonight, tell her she's always welcome here and Suyodhana sends his love!' He then turned his chariot around and joined the Kauravas as they fell back. Bhima looked at his retreating form and threw down his bow in disgust and picked up his mace.

I went over to him and got on his chariot.

'You know he does that purposely to upset you. He wants you to do something stupid.'

He was shaking with rage. 'I'll tear his head off his neck! His tongue out of his face! Bastard!'

We all chose different ways to deal with the loss of our dignity after our humiliation at the sabha. On some level, Arjuna, Nakula, Sahadeva and I had accepted it, and looked towards regaining our kingdom. Our way of avenging our humiliation would be to make Indraprastha the most powerful kingdom in Bharatvarsha. We had learned to live with the taunts. Indeed, deflect them at times with wit.

Thirteen years on, Bhima was the only one who would still physically hurt anyone who dared even suggest anything about Draupadi. He had felt personally responsible for her dignity ever since, and would go to absurd lengths to prove it.

Dignity—it is behind every war fought on the battlefield, the sabha, the playground, the bedroom and the deathbed. We construct an identity around it and defend it till we die. We protect it even when we know we can be better off without it.

I put my arm around my brother as his breath heaved inside his body. He was trying hard not to cry. After a little while, he regained his composure and nudged me away gently. I got back on my chariot and we grinned embarrassedly like only brothers can after a display of emotion.

We took our chariots and joined the rest. The Kauravas had re-formed and were fighting back. Bhagadatta had joined them with a contingent of elephants that were jostling through our ranks. Suyodhana was nowhere to be found.

Bhima went straight for Bhagadatta and was intercepted by an elephant in a purple-and-gold trim and golden armour. The elephant was mounted by a large pavilion, which carried seven archers, three on either side and one in the centre who spoke in a strange tongue. He slapped his thigh and pointed at Bhima and laughed, and spoke some more. He then took out a bow and fired a missile, which barely missed Bhima's charioteer.

This seemed to amuse him and he slapped his thigh again and laughed to the skies and pointed again at Bhima with his palm facing out. He then put a hand on his mahout's shoulder and the elephant charged out if its line into our midst. A strange jingling was heard and I saw the elephant was wearing golden anklets. It created a strange effect. Somewhat like temple bells over a loud aarti.

Bhima jumped out in time, mace in hand, as the elephant overturned the chariot with his trunk. I saw Bhima disappear behind the elephant.

I shouted, 'The bowmen. Kill them,' and a platoon of foot archers gathered around me and fired into the pavilion, killing three of the archers.

Just as we were getting ready to begin work on the elephant, the beast sank on one of its hind feet. And then the other. I saw Bhima at its back, chopping away with his mace. The man in its pavilion was not laughing now.

The remaining archers in the pavilion were brought down by our arrows and Bhima climbed up the elephant triumphantly into the pavilion, holding his mace.

Satyaki's chariot drew near me. He spoke quietly as Bhima lifted his mace and crushed the laughing man's skull, nearly decapitating him with his strength. 'Mlechcha, that one. A foreigner.'

'Really? Where from?'

'Far north. Great king in his land, they say. They call him, called him rather, Arangaa.'

I nodded as Bhima flung King Arangaa's dead body into the

dust and began to pound at the elephant's head with his mace. The elephant's head sank to the ground and its body went still.

Satyaki spoke again, 'I didn't even know that he or his sodding kingdom even existed until he tried to kill me…but I would like to go where they put anklets on elephants. Seems a peaceful kind of place, no?'

Satyaki had a talent for inane conversation so I smiled, but didn't say anything to encourage him.

'I've learned so much from this war. And fighting's the least of it.' He smiled brightly at me and went off.

Bhima beat his chest atop the elephant, drunk on victory. Suyodhana was forgotten for the moment.

And then the elephant toppled over onto its side, anklets jangling. Supritika had rammed into the elephant and was driving it towards our forces like a battering ram. I watched with horror as Bhima lost his footing and fell into the pavilion.

Bhima got up dazed, and before I could shout, he had gone under Supritika.

For the next few moments, I didn't know how to react. My legs buckled and I sat heavily on the floor of my chariot, looking at that monstrosity pushing the elephant carcass into our men. I couldn't think of anything coherent. A thought formed hazily out of a cloud that was my mind. I would have to get Bhima's body. I don't remember getting out of my chariot. I just remember walking blindly towards Supritika with someone pulling back at me. I couldn't tell who.

RADHEYA

Bhima went down like a lily bud in a whirlpool.

Truth is, I didn't know how to feel. A few days back, if someone had told me that Bhima had been killed, I would have been the first at the scene to kick his dead body and spit on it. Maybe second, after Suyodhana.

But now, after my mother's confession regarding my birth, something inside me told me I shouldn't be happy. You aren't supposed to be glad when a little brother dies, are you? But I had hated him for so long. To even begin liking him was shameful.

So, I felt guilt. First, for feeling sorrow, then for correcting my feelings, and trying to feel cheerful. Then, I felt guilty for feeling cheerful. Did I really feel grief at Bhima's death, or was it something I was feeling because I was supposed to? Because it was something that family was supposed to do? Would I feel pain at Suyodhana's death?

I stemmed the flow of questions and thought coldly. I still had to get Yudhishthira and end the war, regardless of Bhima's death. Suyodhana's life could yet be saved. I could still be king. I stopped my thoughts in their path again. It had been two days since my talk with Grandsire, and I realized I still wasn't completely comfortable with the idea of becoming king of the Kurus and taking Suyodhana's kingdom away from him.

King of the Kurus. Would Suyodhana forgive me? Could I forgive myself? Did I even want to become king? Did I want it so that the suta comments would stop? Was I using 'millions of lives can be saved' as an excuse to justify my ambition...?

I yanked my thoughts back again from their meanderings. It could all wait.

I would capture Yudhishthira first and then make a decision. From now, I would not allow myself to feel anything...neither remorse nor joy at any brother's death.

I watched the Pandava morale sink into the blood of Kurukshetra as they tried to get out of Supritika and her dead-elephant-weapon's way. I saw Yudhishthira up front, without a chariot, being held back by four men and Nakula. Now was the time to get him. I pointed my chariots towards the Pandava line and moved us a little distance behind Supritika.

I was about to launch the charge when a Pandava elephant charged at Supritika's flank. Supritika was able to free herself from the elephant carcass just in time to meet the new threat.

The brief distraction made me lose sight of Yudhishthira. I held my chariots back and looked around for him.

The rival was good. He was wearing a simple bronze armour and didn't look like he belonged to any royal family of note. His elephant pushed at Supritika, who pushed back with equal force. There were no feints or lunges or intricate manoeuvres, just tusk thrusts and head butts.

Bhagadatta soon tired of it and picked up a javelin and flung it at the mahout, who was impaled and thrown off the elephant. Old Bloodlust turned around and bowed wickedly. Every Kaurava there whistled and hooted. To throw a javelin was tough enough on land but it was near impossible on a bucking elephant in combat.

Supritika locked tusks and let the mahout-less elephant push at her. Then she took a step back, and let the beast overstep himself. He stumbled forward and she pierced him hard in the side with her tusks. The elephant stumbled and fell and Supritika began goring him in the belly. When she raised her head, entrails hung off her tusk and blood lined her mouth like face paint.

I spotted Yudhishthira in the Pandava ranks being taken back to safer ground. I was about to signal my chariots to move forward when I heard a roar on my right.

The cry of joy had erupted from the Pandava troops. They were holding up Bhima who waved his hand slowly to show that he was still alive.

If I didn't know how to feel when I heard of his death, I was more confused now. So my brother was alive. Should I have been glad? Or upset? Now, getting to Yudhishthira would be as difficult as ever.

I sounded the charge and prayed that Bhima had been injured enough to stay away from the battlefield till we picked up Yudhishthira.

We formed a crescent and charged towards him. Infantry would slow us down, so I had mounted three spearmen on each chariot except mine to give us additional support. There were fifteen Anga chariots. The only ones left after the day's carnage.

A loud trumpet sounded behind us and I saw Supritika coming up in support. A guard hastily made up of Shikhandi, Virata, Nakula and a few other Panchala princes on chariots surrounded Yudhishthira, along with some spearmen.

My chariots began duelling with the Pandava chariots. I killed two Panchala princes and was pierced in the chest by an arrow from Shikhandi.

Grandsire may have had his reservations about fighting women but I could see no wrong in it when the bitch was trying to kill me. Trust the old man to martyr himself for a belief as old as the mountains. I ducked as an arrow missed me narrowly and fired two in retaliation. One hit her on the helmet and the other in the centre of her chest, knocking her down.

Her death could wait. I looked for Yudhishthira, whose chariot lay empty. He had disappeared again. I moved my chariot away from Shikhandi who had still not gotten back on her feet. And began picking off soldiers, searching for Yudhishthira.

Supritika was next to us now and was goring away at a group of Pandava spearmen who were trying to push her back. The fool Satyaki tried to take her head-on and she picked up his chariot like a toy and flung it away, horses and all. Satyaki had the agility to jump off his chariot but his charioteer was not so quick and I heard his cries receding into the distance, ending with a dull crunch.

No sign of Yudhishthira. The Pandavas were growing in numbers around us. We had to move, but advancing towards them was suicide unless I could find him.

I had no choice but to sound a retreat.

I was about to blow the conch when the Pandava forces parted, and a chariot contingent came into view, led by a white chariot with white horses driven by a dark charioteer.

It was Arjuna and he went straight for Supritika who took a step back and swiped at his chariot with her trunk. The chariot swung violently on one wheel and turned away, missing the flailing limb of the elephant. The troops on both sides stood their ground as the chariot and the elephant began their duel.

The cowherd was good with horses. You didn't need to be a charioteer to see that. He feinted in close to her and weaved out without as much as a scratch from her tusks. Frustrated, she snatched at the chariot which spun away. From its back,

Arjuna shot arrows which bounced harmlessly off Supritika's iron armour.

Supritika roared as one of Arjuna's arrows found an unprotected spot between her shoulder and limbs. She charged behind him and tried to gore the fleeing chariot. Krishna swerved and Supritika nearly fell over. She turned around and an arrow hit her straight in her left eye.

I just gaped at Arjuna, who had already loaded another arrow. First Yudhishthira, now Arjuna. Were all the Pandavas targetting eyes today?

I watched dismayed as Supritika went on her knees briefly and whimpered. She got up again, roared and charged straight for the chariot that sped away. Arjuna was firing rapidly trying to find a weak spot.

Bhagadatta cursed and threw a javelin that missed Arjuna's head by a hair's breadth. He flung another one in the middle of the chariot's path as it tried to escape. The chariot swerved around the javelin and went around to the elephant's flank.

Supritika turned and followed. Arjuna fired four arrows, all at the head. His chariot turned away from her path again and Arjuna fired at the head once more.

I saw his plan. Supritika's earlier combat with the war elephant had cracked her skull plate. Arjuna was trying to expose it, or put an arrow between it. I shouted at Bhagadatta, 'The head! He's going for the head!'

The old king didn't hear me and picked up another javelin.

Arjuna continued to put arrows into Supritika's skull till finally she stopped, exhausted.

A thin stream of blood was dripping to the ground from her head. Bhagadatta made her sit. She tried to pull out an arrow and nearly peeled off half the skull plate. The arrows were barbed and stuck firm to her skin and the plate. To remove the arrows was to remove the armour, which was already coming out in pieces.

While Supritika wrestled with the arrows, Bhagadatta brought out his bow and fired at Arjuna, who twisted away from the dart and fired back, shattering Bhagadatta's bow and taking a finger.

The elephant king tied his hand calmly with a silk cloth and patted his elephant soothingly. The chariot charged at them again, Arjuna firing arrow after arrow into Supritika's head. The armour was in tatters and hung limply on her forehead. The elephant struggled back on her feet and roared. She swung her head wildly from side to side and charged straight at the chariot. Krishna swerved the vehicle out of her path even as Arjuna fired an arrow that went clean through her eye.

Supritika fell.

Even in death she had the presence of mind to fall first on her knees and skid to a halt so that Bhagadatta wouldn't be thrown off.

The chariot came around to face Bhagadatta. The old king was wiping the tears from his eyes and rubbing Supritika on the head to gently guide her passage into the next world. He saw the chariot and lowered his head in defeat. For a moment, both Arjuna and Krishna relaxed and Bhagadatta chose that moment to lift his elephant goad and throw it at Arjuna. Krishna stood up and took the blow on his chest. Bhagadatta brought out a javelin and threw it. Arjuna pushed Krishna out of the way and the javelin nicked Arjuna's arm, bloodying his white-and-silver armour.

Arjuna turned and fired an arrow. It sheared through Bhagadatta's helmet, forcing him to tear it off his head. The silk kerchief that he wore to soak up the sweat fell over his face, blinding him.

Arjuna's next arrow pierced his forehead.

The old king fell back onto his elephant.

I was glad that the kerchief had covered his face. I wouldn't have been able to see him dead.

A roar broke out from the Pandava forces and they rushed towards Arjuna. Our troops, shocked after seeing the death of Supritika and Bhagadatta, panicked.

The troops around me broke formation and began to run. I pulled out my conch and blasted the signal to hold the line. This wasn't having any effect so I started shouting at the troops, telling them to stand and withdraw in an orderly manner.

The Pandava troops must have seen this, for they began advancing, their bowmen firing into ours, who were running in terror.

I retreated further, trying to rally the men even as Arjuna led the Pandava advance. While everyone was running to some kind of safety, two chariots from our lines headed towards the Pandavas. They were Vrisha and Achala, Shakuni's brothers, followed by a squadron of Kamboja cavalry.

I shouted at them to turn back, but they didn't listen. Soon, it was just them against the Pandava advance. Arjuna personally made quick work of them. An arrow went through Vrisha's throat and another pierced Achala's heart. The Kambojas were swallowed instantly by the Pandava onslaught.

Next, Shakuni's chariot went past me towards the Pandavas. I saw his face, white with fear, as he went looking for his brothers and found them dead. He took up his bow in a rage and began firing into the Pandava front. He would have been killed but for a surviving Kamboja rider who lifted him off his chariot onto his horse and brought him back.

I heard a conch peal and looked behind me. Fresh Kaurava troops had formed together in a perfect line to hold the Pandava charge. They let the retreating soldiers pass between them and held their weapons at the ready.

At their head was Drona.

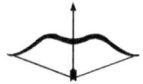

THE TWELFTH NIGHT

YUDHISHTHIRA

I entered the council tent and the conversation stopped. Virata and Drupada were not present. They would join us soon, I was told. The seats were arranged in a circle; Arjuna, Nakula, Chekitana and Sahadeva made one semi-circle and I took the seat to the right of Arjuna. To my right was Shikhandi, who sat next to Dhristadyumna. Two seats were left empty for Virata and Drupada and next to them sat Bhima. Apart from a few bruises on his arms he looked fit.

As soon as I sat down, he came to me, kneeled, put a hand on my shoulder and said, 'I'm fine.'

I touched his face and smiled.

He took his place. The council tent found its voices again. Arjuna spoke to young Chekitana. Nakula and Sahadeva were listening intently. Shikhandi and Dhristadyumna began discussing something.

Krishna pulled up a chair and sat next to me.

'A difficult day, but a good one...in the larger scheme of things.'

I nodded. I didn't know what to say. The day had left its scars on me. The sooner it was forgotten, the sooner they would heal. I had shamed myself in front of everyone by reacting the way I did. It had taken Nakula and four guards to physically restrain me from going out and searching for Bhima. It was only when Radheya's chariots began their charge that I realized that I was still in the middle of the battle.

I was seeing Bhima for the first time after the battle. When Supritika rammed into the dead elephant, he had fallen between Supritika's tusks and the elephant's body. Luckily he fell on his feet and narrowly missed being stepped on by Supritika. He had then caught her by the belly strap and hung on till he was able to drop safely into a pile of carcasses where he lay until our men found him.

Krishna continued, 'Bhagadatta's death is a big one.'

'Where did you learn to drive a chariot like that?' I asked, trying to change the discussion.

'Here and there.'

'Here and there? You were dancing around her.'

'I was lucky. It could just as well have been her day.'

Virata's arrival interrupted our conversation. His eyes were red but without tears. His son Ketama had been killed today. Drupada came in soon after. He had lost sons as well. The tent grew silent and we waited for Dhristadyumna to begin.

He cleared his throat and spoke, 'For the most part, the day, er, went our way. Arjuna killed Lord Bhagadatta. Drona was injured.'

I looked down as he spoke, hoping that my incident would not be brought up in the council. That it would die a quiet, lonely death out on the battlefield and be forgotten.

'Yudhishthira...'

Damn.

'What happened today?'

I looked at the floor as I spoke.

'I don't know. I lost my senses...for a little while...when I heard the rumour of Bhima's death.'

He stood silent for a moment. I saw Virata's mouth twist into a grimace of disgust as he looked away. Dhristadyumna continued to look at me and spoke again softly:

'That's not what, what I was referring to.'

I looked at the faces of everyone in the council and could find no answer in their eyes.

'It is, um, understandable to be upset after a personal loss... to lose your power to reason. It happens to us all. It was fortunate that Nakula was around to bring you back to safety.'

I saw Virata shake his head viciously and rasp, 'You're a warrior, you little sod. You're supposed to control your emotions in a fight. Fine leader of the Kurus you'll be.'

I looked at Virata's eyes glaring at me. He had spoken my mind. But I continued to look him in the eyes to show that I was not scared.

Dhristadyumna interrupted the old king, 'My Lord, please let me continue. Yudhishthira, you don't need me to lecture you on how to deal with grief. As long as no lives were lost, I am content.'

He turned back and looked at Virata and then at me, and said in a low voice, 'But what upset me today, Yudhishthira, was your willingness to get off your chariot and surrender to Drona when he had you cornered.'

I had completely forgotten about that.

The silence in the tent grew louder. Dhristadyumna's soft voice amplified like thunder.

'Yudhishthira, we are all here fighting for you and your brothers. If you can abandon your own cause so easily, there is no sense continuing this war. I would like to make terms with Kauravas tonight and end this bloodshed on Kurukshetra.'

Bhima stood up with clenched fists and said, 'Dhristadyumna, don't talk like a fool.'

Arjuna turned towards me and said, 'Yudhishthira?'

Nakula, Sahadeva and Chekitana, as the youngest members of the council, stayed seated but looked earnestly at me for an explanation.

Old Virata threw his hands up in disgust.

The only ones who didn't react were Drupada, who was massaging his thigh, and Krishna, who looked keenly at the floor.

I was angry at the suggestion of cowardice; at the notion that we couldn't win the war without his troops; at the practised coldness of his words.

No one knew what was going through my mind when I stepped off the chariot.

If Dhristadyumna wanted to play games, I was ready.

'Dhristadyumna, it saddens me that you have such little faith in me or the cause of my family that you would be willing to go over to the other side because of the events of one day. If you are accusing me of cowardice, of abandoning my own cause, as you say so bluntly, then you are twisting my intentions to serve your own. Let me clarify for the council, which consists of all the people I hold in the greatest regard on this earth. Yes, Guru Drona had cornered me. Despite the valiant attempts of your own Panchala princes. And yes, I had gotten off my chariot. But it was to distract him and end his onslaught and give our men a chance to rally. It doesn't matter if I am captured and even killed. The war will, and must, go on.

'Do you think I would make war on my family? Fight for a cause so terrible without understanding its repercussions? If you don't know this by now you can take your army and leave the field. This was no way to talk to an ally, to humiliate him in front of a war council.'

He hadn't expected this. He had thought I'd be on my knees saying, 'Oh, forgive me, commander-in-chief, sir, not everyone can be as brave and upright and honest and strong like you. Don't leave us and go.'

But I wasn't done yet.

'And Dhristadyumna, all of this would never have happened if you had planned your trap better. Did you really think that a few Panchala children and you had any real chance with Drona?'

I got up from my seat, swung my shawl across my shoulder in defiance and began to walk out. Drupada intercepted my path. I regarded him and he smiled sadly at me.

'Son, it's been a long day for us all.'

He took me by the hand and walked me over to Dhristadyumna, who was breathing heavily.

'We are not allies here. We are family. I have faith that Yudhishthira wouldn't run away from our fight, just as I have faith that you, Dhristadyumna, wouldn't take a decision that didn't benefit us all. That is the end of the matter. It is time to forgive each other.'

He nudged a resisting and reluctant Dhristadyumna towards me. He nudged again, a little harder this time, and Dhristadyumna extended his hand hesitatingly. I took it and we hugged each other briefly. Both of us sat down in our places and did not say a word to each other for the rest of the council.

I walked back to my tent with Bhima. We didn't talk much, but as we approached my tent, I remembered, 'Bhima, what were you thinking, duelling with bows with Suyodhana?'

He paused and replied, 'I don't know. He had his out, so I got mine. I didn't think too much about it.'

I didn't say anything. After a while, he spoke, 'Did you see the shot?'

'Yes. It was very lucky.'

He slapped me affectionately on the back.

We stopped in front of my tent. He was serious now. 'Yudhishthira, you don't need to answer this. But I want to know.'

I nodded, already knowing the question.

He whispered, so that even the wind wouldn't hear, 'Did you...were you really going to surrender to Guruji?'

'As I said in the council, it was done deliberately to end his assault on our forces.'

He smiled with pursed lips and hugged me.

I wondered what he'd have said if I had told him that I'd given in to my panic and obeyed Guruji because it was the easiest thing to do at that moment. That all I really wanted was for the war to be over. For all of us to stop pretending that killing each other would make things better. For life to resume.

I don't think he'd have believed me.

We were all pretenders here. Pretenders to our families Pretenders in the eyes of our enemies. Pretenders in the words of our bards.

Pretenders to ourselves.

RADHEYA

The retreat had been terrible. Everyone lost their nerve, including some of the senior commanders, I heard. We had lost more men in the stampede towards our lines than by Pandava hands. It had taken the sight of Drona and half the reserves to slow them down.

On the other side of the field, the Trigartas had been quite successful initially and had even penetrated the main Pandava force until Arjuna had pushed them back.

The wind was fast and chilly. It slapped the tiredness out of my head. Bhagadatta was finally gone. A long fight and a quick death. He would've have liked it, I think. He was always good to me. Never called me names or anything.

I said a small prayer for the fire-breather and his elephant, hoping they were together somewhere with the old man boozing and whoring his way for eternity.

I entered my tent and ate a bone of chicken with some bread and a bowl of lentils. I then lay down on my bed and let my masseur pummel my body into surrender.

I must have dozed off for he was not there when I woke up. I heard a loud commotion outside and went to the entrance of my tent to see what was going on.

It was Supritika. The armour was in tatters around her forehead and the blood was pouring, thick and black, out of her skull. She swayed and tottered and roared and, picking up a soldier, threw him away like a scarecrow. The camp behind her was burning. Where her left eye should have been was a bloody socket. She trampled into the tents, crushing its inhabitants, whose screams were muffled by the cloth. She trumpeted again, and shook her head. Her blood flew and splattered me in the eyes. I wiped my face only to see her charging towards me, bellowing with rage. I tried to run but I stood stuck to the spot. The beast charged into me.

And I woke up breathing heavily.

It was late evening and nearly time for the council. I asked a servant to draw a hot bath, and after a quick wash, put on a clean dhoti and draped a shawl around myself and walked towards the council tent.

I met Varahamira on the way, and took him to a corner.

'Everyone's miserable, sire. No one's talking. It's worse than when Lord Bhishma left the field. I hear they've delayed the council meeting because of it.'

It was true. The tent was empty. I went and sat inside and waited for someone to come.

It took a little while. I had just begun to think of going to Suyodhana's tent when our first allies trickled in. And then some more. There was sadness in their eyes. Not the kind that comes with grief, but with helplessness. Drona walked in with Suyodhana, followed by Shakuni. His eyes were swollen and his beard was wet with tears.

He looked at me and spat, 'Coward.' And walked away before I knew what happened.

Everyone took their places and Drona picked up the Speaking Staff.

'Today was one of the worst days I have ever had on the field. We have just shown our backs to our enemy. Run from them like petrified hens. We have shown them that we fear them. Worse, that we will run away when are afraid. Yes, I don't see Bhishma here today, or Lord Bhagadatta. But other than the two of them, I see all the men who won us the first eight days of the war. I want you to remember that as you go back to your tents today and come back with your strength and courage for tomorrow's battle.'

Drona sat down and Shakuni charged and picked up the staff. He looked at the council and hissed, 'Fine words, Guruji, fine words indeed. These aren't men, they are rats. Vermin. There were only two men out there today and they were killed because of these cowards. Vrishala and Achala. Remember their names, scum.'

Shakuni shook the staff and then pounded it on the ground screaming their names. No one dared interrupt him till Suyodhana caught him by his shoulders and pinned him down. The Speaking Staff slipped from Shakuni's grip and rolled towards me. I went over, picked it up and waited for the commotion to end.

I had to take matters in hand.

Shakuni was escorted out of the tent still a little disoriented. I waited for everyone to settle in their positions and spoke, 'Drona, your strategy has been bad from the beginning. We haven't captured Yudhishthira yet. Nor have we killed any of the Pandavas. We need a new plan. Something that's a little less defensive...and a little less outdated.'

It was sacrilege. Up there with mixing sura in a sage's water bottle. To question strategy was one thing. To question Drona personally was quite another. However, I was not scared.

'I'm not done, Drona. It's bad enough that you hatched your little plan in secret with Susharma. He went out and announced it to the fucking world.'

Susharma stood up. 'Unlike you, I'm not a coward. I fear

no one, not even Arjuna.'

'Susharma, sit down. This is not about you.'

He sat down slowly, still glaring at me.

I looked at the room.

'This is about all of us. We're allies. We deserve to know the battle strategy in full, before the day starts. Now tell us, Drona, why weren't we informed?'

He rose to the bait.

'I am the commander-in-chief of this army. It's my decision. How dare you question it, suta?'

Suyodhana walked up to me and asked for the staff. I gave it to him reluctantly.

'What Radheya says is correct, Guruji. We must trust each other as allies. That means we can't keep key elements of strategy hidden. It shouldn't happen again in the future.'

Drona nodded stiffly.

The rest of the allies nodded too, relieved that Suyodhana had said what was running through all their minds.

'And another thing. Radheya is the king of Anga. From now on, no one in this council will refer to him as anything other than *Lord* Radheya.'

Drona didn't react. The other allies looked at the ground, avoiding each other's glances.

Suyodhana continued, 'The day is past now. And I still believe Guruji is the best battle commander in this room.'

He looked at me when he said that. His eyes hoping I wouldn't contradict him.

'But I also believe we need a different way of fighting the enemy now that our most experienced fighters are gone.'

He looked at Drona and said, 'Guruji, you need to think

of a new strategy.'

For a moment, I almost felt sorry for Drona. It was like asking a man to invent the wheel without telling him what it was needed for.

He almost choked on his words as he said them, 'Putra, there is nothing wrong with my strategy. We have been a little unfortunate in its execution, that's all. Nothing that we won't be able to put right tomorrow.'

Suyodhana expected a better answer than that. 'Guruji, it's obvious there is some flaw in your approach. Otherwise we'd be winning, right?'

'Formations alone don't win battles, putra.'

'Then tell me, Guruji, what does?'

'This conversation is futile.'

'What will win us this battle, Guruji? What are we doing wrong?'

'Sometimes, putra, everything can go right, and we can still lose the battle. We have to just keep doing everything right till we begin to win.'

'That's not good enough, Guruji. Tell me how we can win through tomorrow or let me appoint a commander-in-chief who can.'

Had I been in Drona's place, I would have walked out of the tent, out of Kurukshetra.

Drona let the insult pass and merely said, 'There is no need. I will have a plan tomorrow.'

Suyodhana nodded.

'Thank you, Guruji. And if you're not able to get us Yudhishthira tomorrow, we'll appoint a commander-in-chief who will.'

Drona replied, 'Then I don't have much time,' and walked out of the tent.

The meeting ended almost immediately after that, with Suyodhana telling the allies to get some rest.

I waited for the crowd to leave the tent and approached Suyodhana.

'You showed the old bugger that you mean business.'

'Please don't call him that.'

He turned away from me and stormed off towards his tent. As he left, I heard him tell his retainer, 'Double rations for the troops today. Inform the cooks.'

I walked a few paces towards my own and stopped. A thought struck me. Sleep could wait.

It was cool on the twelfth night of Kurukshetra but the fires in Drona's tent were still burning late at night. I entered the tent unannounced. It was bare and would have resembled a foot soldier's tent with its cheap leather hide and pock-marked tent poles were it not for the royal insignia displayed on the tent's entrance. The old prude refused any 'indulgences' in times of war and slept on a wooden plank with his mattress rolled up into a rough pillow. The tent itself had been a recent addition because Suyodhana had insisted that it wouldn't be appropriate for the commander of his armies to sleep out in the open.

He was sitting on the plank and reading when I entered.

'Didn't you learn to ask for permission before entering a tent?'

His eyes burned through me like hot ghee through a soft chapati. After forty years of living a life hardened by the military ambitions of his students, he had an uncanny knack of making everyone feel like they were under inspection. I had heard that on one occasion, a minor king of an eastern principality had even fainted on his wedding day, after being the subject of Drona's gaze. For a moment, I pitied Ashwatthama his childhood. No wonder he was such a surly lout.

'They don't teach us these niceties in the stable, sire.'

'Sire? Well now, what happened to "Drona"? You have come to mock me, haven't you? Get out!'

'I'm here to help you…sire.'

'You little toad. What makes you think I'll need your help? Come back tomorrow and fight. And don't run away. That will be enough.'

'I have an idea. A strategy of sorts. It may work.'

'Don't talk to me about leading armies, boy; I've been winning campaigns before your father had learned to clean horses.'

'Maybe so, sire, but the nature of war has changed over the past hundred years. Maybe what this war really needs is someone who can come up with a strategy that's not written in an ancient text.'

That silenced him for a moment. He thought a little and returned to verbal fencing.

'So, tell me this "original" plan of yours; the one that has no precedent. Has it even been tested in battle?'

'Let me answer your questions one by one. Yes, it's original. No, it's not mine. No, it hasn't been studied at military colleges. And last, it's not *a* formation. It's formations, actually. Two of them together.'

'Two? Do you know how hard it is to get soldiers to make one formation, much less switch to another? Two formations in one day? Can you hear yourself talk?'

'Two formations, sire. Both of them fighting at the same time.'

That got his attention. He motioned me to sit next to him. From the folds of his dhoti, he removed a small apple, which he cut with a small knife and popped a slice in his mouth and offered me a piece.

We spoke till late that night. And when I left, we were not friends, but we were no longer enemies.

Someone was sitting on a chair outside my tent, draped in a shawl. He was trying unsuccessfully to stay awake. His head lolled to the side, his back relaxed and he nearly fell off the chair. He corrected his posture and sat upright again, shaking sleep out of his head.

I walked up to him and put my hand on his shoulder. It was Laxman.

He got up hastily, 'Sorry, sire, I didn't see you coming.'

'Why are you here so late, putra?'

'Nothing, sire. I wanted to talk, if you're not tired.'

'Not at all. Come.'

We went into my tent and I poured a hot honey decoction in brass tumblers for both of us. I sat at my writing desk while he pulled a chair next to me and occupied it. He came to the point, 'Sire, I want to fight with the Samsaptakas tomorrow. I can't speak of it to Father because he'll tell me to follow my battle orders. A word from you could perhaps...'

'Perhaps?'

'Well, maybe convince him otherwise.'

I suddenly felt very tired. I didn't want to hear about battle anymore. Placements, formations, numbers, deployments.

'I'll think about it. You fought today, didn't you?'

'Yes sire.'

'And?'

'I killed two chariot warriors. Panchala, I think.'

'Why the Samsaptakas?'

He took a deep breath before he said the next words, 'I'll have a better chance of finding Arjuna with them.'

To think that he could match Arjuna when Bhishma, Bhagadatta, Shalya and Drona hadn't! I was too tired to shout at him or smack him with my sandal.

'Arjuna? Wait in line. There are at least a hundred better warriors ahead of you who would be glad for a duel with him. Myself included.'

'I didn't mean to suggest...'

'I know. And there's nothing wrong with wanting the glory of his blood on your hands either. But you'll have to wait for your turn. When all of us have failed you will have your chance.'

He pursed his lips, nodded and left with a cold 'Thank you, sire'.

I soaked a piece of linen in some water and put it on my eyes.

How did it ever come to this?

Ah, yes.

Lady Kunti had asked to see me on the day before I left for the war. We would meet at a temple in the evening. Neutral ground.

I went out of curiousity. It couldn't be a trap. The Pandavas would never use their mother as bait for an assassination. They'd be laughed out of Bharatvarsha.

The temple was an old stone structure dedicated to the Sun God. The evening prayers had just been completed and the priests were finishing for the day. She sat waiting for me on the temple steps.

I offered my namaskaram and got to the point.

'You asked me here, Lady Kunti. What can I do for you?'

She looked at my face for a long time.

'Putra,' she said at last.

I bowed my head.

'Radheya, you are my son.'

Had the old lady gone senile?

'I know, I know. It's a little late to be telling you this. But now is as good a time as any. You were born to me. The son of...well, a king. Let's leave it at that. How can I prove it? Your father must have told you that he found you in a red-coloured box, wearing golden earrings. Did he not? I had bundled you in a gold cloth as well.'

She continued, 'You have two birthmarks. One on your forearm as anyone can see. And the other just below your navel.'

She was right. Both about how Father had found me and my birthmarks. She could have got the information on the birthmarks from any number of women in Hastinapura, but the stuff about my birth was something only Father knew.

Her spies were good.

Or she was telling the truth.

I sat down a little distance from her.

'Okay, you seem to know a lot about me. If what you say is true, what do you want from me...Mother?'

She sighed.

'I didn't expect you to take this seriously. I just want you to know that I am sorry for abandoning you, putra. I don't expect you to feel any love for me. But I want to let you know that the house of the Pandavas is yours whenever you choose to come to it.'

The words were in my head, but they took some time coming down out of my mouth.

'Do my brothers know?'

'No one knows, except your foster father Adiratha, whom I swore to secrecy, my brother Vidura and Grandsire Bhishma.'

Perfect. My now foster father was not alive, and I was not on talking terms with Grandsire. We had clashed a number of times in the lead up to the battle over minor issues. Finally, his stubbornness to listen to my point of view had led me to remove myself from the field of battle as long as he was on it.

'Mother' continued, 'I was not married. As you know, to have a child out of wedlock is unacceptable. I was young and only looking to protect myself. Adiratha offered to take you off my hands.'

'He told me he found me floating in the Yamuna. I had always found it a little hard to believe.'

She went quiet again.

Finally she started.

'I'm sorry for all the sadness in your life that has come because of me. As a mother, all I can ask of you is that you show some mercy to your brothers in the war.'

'I'll try.'

What else could I say? That I was going to hunt down every one of her sons and give them a painful end?

I gave her a namaskaram and walked away without looking back.

ABHIMANYU

My shoulder had received a light cut, nothing that wouldn't heal in a couple of days. Another scar ran across my thigh like a road wrapped around a mountain. A Trigarta had slashed down with his scimitar and ripped my dhoti as I twisted away from its arc. The curved blade kissed my skin very briefly but was enough to bloody it and leave a line running around my leg. Other than that I was fine.

If Father was to be believed, I had almost died.

I was furious with him after he had interfered in my battle with the Trigarta platoon. I told Sumitra to overtake his chariot into their lines. We charged with all the pace the horses could muster and broke through their front, running over many of them. My bow was out and I fired at anything I could find. I soon realized my mistake because we were isolated, with no support either from chariots or the infantry. I removed an axe and hacked at the Trigarta infantry who howled and tried jumping onto the chariot that was moving as fast as Sumitra and the horses could make it. Our progress began to slow. Sumitra finally turned us around to retreat and was nearly impaled by a javelin that smashed through the chariot rim and would have taken my crotch had I not skipped sideways. A Trigarta tried to step on the chariot plank and I planted a blow on his head for his effort. Another one ran side by side with us till I cleaved his neck with a side stroke.

At this point, the warrior with the scimitar entered the scene. He stepped onto the running chariot and slashed wildly at my thigh. He wasn't able to finish the job as an arrow took him in the back of his head. He slunk to the ground mouthing some nonsense and I kicked him off.

Father had arrived. And just in time too. His chariot troop had formed a neat diamond and was discharging arrows with arithmetic precision. Father's skill with the bow was known in every gutter of Bharatvarsha. He had shot a fish suspended fifty feet in the air, in the eye, by looking at its reflection in the water, so the story went. I had tried to perform the same stunt and had never succeeded. In my childhood, I used to believe that the fact that he drew the bow with his left hand was the reason he was able to shoot so accurately, and had spent many nights secretly lifting weights with my left hand, trying to strengthen it till Krishna caught me in the act.

'Don't make your weaknesses weaker. Make your strengths stronger, child,' he had told me, ruffling my hair and setting down the weight-training mace in the training pit.

His words came back as I saw Father shoot a Trigarta, who was a sword's strike away from him, in the face. I had never seen him fight with anything but a bow. To engage him in close combat was rare because he was just too fast with the bow. Only on one occasion had I seen him swing his bow like a staff, at an axeman who had gotten too close. He never carried any weapon other than several quivers of arrows, which he would run through like a depressed poet through parchment. It wasn't uncommon for him to ask for quiverfuls of arrows from nearby chariots when his own supply was depleted. Father had taken his single strength and had amplified it beyond measure, till it did not matter what his other deficiencies were.

He went past me without a glance in my direction. The king of the Trigartas charged towards him on his chariot, firing arrows in his general direction, but with no real accuracy. Father dodged them with little effort and when they were a horse's-length away from each other, he brought out a flat-headed arrow with no point, and shot him square in the face.

The Trigarta king fell out of his chariot as it rattled by. A group of soldiers picked him up and dragged him back to safety.

Just when Father was about to hunt him out, a courier rode into their midst. He stopped with great effort and panted out a message to Father. Father spoke briefly to Uncle Sahadeva who was nearby, and made his way out to the back. Uncle took his place and resumed the attack. They wouldn't call Father back unless there was something seriously wrong in another sector. I was tempted to join him, but thought against it. There were enough people to kill out here.

I regretted it later when I found out that he had gone and killed old Bhagadatta and saved our flank from being overwhelmed by the Kauravas.

I was kicking myself in my tent when he came in and began scolding me. He had called me impatient and went on about waiting for my chance and not learning anything from yesterday. I nodded dully and assured him of my obedience. He walked away disgusted.

It was all right for him to talk. The bards would be making money off him for centuries. Stories about him that we didn't even know about were already being sung. And that was all before the Kurukshetra war. If we won here on these plains, he would be famous for eternity.

I took a walk to clear my head. The evening breeze was cool. The sky was purple and torches would not be needed for some more time. I found myself drifting towards Shikhandi's tent yet again. She would know what to do.

'Do what they tell you to,' was her simple advice.

She was writing a letter and didn't look up when she said this.

'I am, aren't I? It's not working. I don't see why they can't use me better.'

This made her stop writing and look up.

'You poor little child hero with no one to kill. Whatever's going to happen to you?'

'Stop that. You don't understand. I should never have come.'

I turned to exit when she spoke.

'Don't play victim with me, Abhimanyu. And don't think I don't know how you or any of the young fools in the army feel about proving themselves. All I'm saying is, there is a journey. You need to prove yourself in the eyes of your elders and superiors. You need to prove that you will not be a threat to their ambitions. That you will follow their instructions without succumbing to your own, at this point insignificant, emotions. Once you have done that, you will have come of age—when you become what *they* want you to become. And only then will you be given the freedom to do what you want.'

'What you're saying is that I should just become a toy soldier, winded up and played with at someone else's whim?'

'You don't have to be anything you don't want, Abhi. But you have to accept that the only way you will get your chance is by keeping the people around you happy.'

I shrugged and walked out.

I didn't need her cynicism. I wondered what had ever

possessed me to seek comfort from her. With nothing left to do, I went back into my tent.

I wrote some rubbish to Mother and went to bed.

THE THIRTEENTH DAY

RADHEYA

My eyes opened. They took in the ceiling of the tent and my brain goaded my body out of bed. A cold bath with tulsi leaves got the blood cantering.

Summons had been sent late last night for an early-morning council meeting. I walked quickly to the tent and was pleasantly surprised to find that I was the last one in. Drona held a cup of steaming liquid in his hand and was talking animatedly to Suyodhana. They appeared calmer than yesterday. Shakuni sat in a corner munching a piece of jaggery, not talking to anyone. He looked better too.

I went up to Drona and he smiled tiredly at me...for the first time, perhaps ever.

'We were waiting for you, putra. Let's begin.'

He took the Speaking Staff and knocked it on the ground till everyone was looking at him.

'For the past two days, I have been blamed for the failure of this army.'

The allies began to protest.

'No, no. It's true. Settle down. Till yesterday, it was claimed my formations were not strong enough or smart enough to outmanoeuvre the Pandavas.'

Now, they stood silent, not knowing how to react.

'I'd like to see anyone say that today.'

He paused for effect, and began again.

'Today, we shall split our forces. One half, under King Susharma, will consist of the Trigartas, the Kambojas, Gandharas and the northern tribes along with the tribes from the east. They will occupy our left flank, formed as a crescent. Susharma, like yesterday, your job will be to draw out Arjuna and keep him occupied. We'll have to work on that personal challenge of yours. Remind me before we get on the field.'

'Arjuna will make his way to the left and divide their forces. This is where the the fun begins. The right flank, till then, will be a wall of shields which will conceal troop movements behind it. When the battle starts they will break away and run to the back. Behind them will be a second formation.'

He rolled out a diagram and showed it to the allies.

'It's called the Chakravyuha. Radheya, will you come and talk about this, please.'

I slowly walked up to Drona and took the staff from him. He patted me on the back as he released it.

'Thank you, sire. The vyuha is the work of obscure military theorists who have tried to conceive a new way of deploying forces. Not too many people have read about it. I myself chanced upon a manuscript of it at a raid in the southern territories a year or so back. I completely forgot about it, till last night.

'Imagine an onion. Now see it peeled, unravelling layer after layer till the centre is exposed. And you have the basic principle behind the Chakravyuha. The formation is a circular one. The outermost layer will have a shield wall of infantry that will protect chariots carrying archers positioned behind them.

'This will spiral into another layer made up similarly. All together there will be seven concentric layers around the centre.

As they march forward, the troops will be ordered, every few minutes, to take seven steps to their right. This will make the vyuha appear as if it's turning in a circle like a wheel, disorienting our enemies.'

I paused here and waited for them to catch up.

'The outermost layer will have an opening to let the enemy troops into the vyuha. When they enter, we will grind them piecemeal. The only way for the enemy to exit each layer of the vyuha would be to punch through it, which will take them into another layer. Followed by another, and another, wearing them down till there is no more left of them.

'One more thing—elephants will be kept in reserve today. This is a delicate formation that cannot be ruined by clumsy trampling.'

I looked at the faces. They were calculating their potential losses, no doubt.

'Questions?'

A king from a southern kingdom raised his hand. I flung the staff towards him.

'Is there a way to counter this formation? And would the Pandavas know about it?'

'There is only one way to break the vyuha. And that is from the inside. We have to clamp off as many of their troops as possible at each layer and not allow them to reach the centre. If they are able to send a steady stream of troops into our centre, they will be able to rip us open. Imagine a thumb in an orange. As for the Pandavas knowing how to tackle the formation, to the best of my knowledge, Arjuna may know of its existence. But not in any great detail for sure. Shalya here claims that he mentioned it casually a couple of times to him when the families were at peace. I know for certain that if he knew about it in any detail, they would have used it on us ten days ago.'

This was welcomed by laughter.

'But whether or not he knows, there's no reason we should take a chance. That is why Susharma and his Trigartas and the others will have to occupy his attention and pin him and his akshauhinis down till the Chakravyuha rolls up the Pandava flank like a blanket. Once this is done, we'll hit Arjuna's forces from the side, and he won't have the numbers to counter us.'

Another hand went up. The staff was passed over.

'Do we still capture Yudhishthira?'

I had discussed this with Drona last night.

'It's imprudent to waste three days trying to capture one man,' he had said.

'Not if it ends the war,' I had argued. 'I saw the bills this morning. Our expenditure on food itself will run us into debt for the next ten years. We can't wait till the death of every one of us. We have to win this now.'

He'd scratched his beard.

'We haven't been able to do it for two days. With everyone, you, me, Suyodhana, even Bhagadatta, taking their best chance. What makes you think we can do it tomorrow?'

I'd shrugged. 'It's a new formation. It may bring us luck.'

He had smiled wryly but I continued, 'Once he's in the vyuha layers, he's ours.'

'Fine. Then let's make a deal. If he enters the vyuha, we'll take him alive. But I don't want anyone breaking the formation to go and get him. Clear?'

Now I looked at the king who had asked the question and nodded. 'Yes. But today, we won't go after him like we did yesterday or the day before. If he gets close, we'll draw him into our layers. When he is in, give your troops strict instructions to take him alive.'

I looked at our allies, waiting for another question.

After an adequate duration, Suyodhana took the staff from me and spoke to the council.

'I'm convinced. Completely. I asked Guruji to try a new formation and he's given us something that no one's ever heard of.'

He looked at the council and boomed, 'Shall we go ahead? Or does anyone have a better plan?'

Some of the allies smiled. They appeared somewhat convinced. If not of the plan, at least of the attempt to try something different. A good sign.

I handed the staff over to Drona who gave everyone their positions. The seven layers would be under the charge of our minor allies to keep everyone equally responsible for our defeat, should it happen. Shalya, Suyodhana, Ashwatthama, Drona, Kritavarma, a few more Maharathis and I would float between layers and bolster any division that needed help. The front line would be managed by the Sindhu king, Jayadratha. It would have the most diffficult task of the day—to contain the Pandava assault and also act as a gate to let them in.

We had discussed this at length, Drona and I. Apart from Suyodhana and his brothers and the Trigartas, Jayadratha was probably the only king who had a personal enmity with the Pandavas. Like the Trigartas, we would put his anger to good use.

All of us left the tent together. The sun had just risen. Susharma walked away with Drona and Suyodhana walked energetically towards his tent, barking orders jovially to his menials. I hadn't seen him so excited since the first few days. Another good sign.

I returned to my tent and hastily put on my armour.

As I left for the chariot park, I saw a dove fly slowly across our camp, stretching out its wings and welcoming the waking sun. It was a strange sight for a battlefield but was an auspicious sign. This was too good to be true. I reminded myself not to get carried away. When had anything ever gone well on the field?

When I reached the field, it had already been arranged just like we had planned. The white of the Trigartas rimmed the crescent on the left. On the right, a solid shield wall protected the Chakravyuha that was under construction. When everyone had finally taken their positions, Suyodhana spoke quietly in the centre, and his message was carried to every member in the ranks.

'By now, all of you know what is required of you. So I won't speak of battle. I will speak to you instead of dinner. Now some of you may have noticed double rations on your plate yesterday night. Some may even have thought it a mistake. I don't think anyone bothered to correct it. Am I right?'

The ranks were silent. I saw a long-spearman look nervously at the soldiers on his side from the corner of his eyes.

'Let me confirm. It was not a mistake. But your due.'

It took every moment of every year of the spearman's discipline not to turn around and look at Suyodhana.

'Yesterday, we were hammered. Some of us even ran from the carnage. For a while, I didn't know who to blame. And I still don't. But I know in my heart that I cannot blame you.'

The spearman looked straight ahead now. His eyebrows sloped in puzzlement.

'I speak to you as individuals. To each one of you. You are the best soldiers any army can ask for. And after proving your strength, resolve and loyalty time and again for twelve days straight, I'm ashamed that I brought it to a point that it could no longer be tested. But today is a new day. We have a new plan. We are arranged in a new vyuha. And all I ask is that each of you continues to make me feel that I belong to the greatest army on earth by standing and fighting like the heroes you are. Today is the thirteenth day. Today is the day we win the war.'

The army erupted. The spearman tightened his grip on the spear.

YUDHISHTHIRA

The council meeting was brief. All we had from our spies was hearsay and gossip. Some talk of a new battle formation which we rubbished immediately. Soldiers' tales...they could give the bards a run for their money. I had heard of flying vehicles, explosive arrows called astras that could destroy entire akshauhinis and a great deal more. If we took everything they said seriously we would be preparing for the apocalypse at every little skirmish.

Dhristadyumna arranged us in staggered squares. From the sky the army would look like checks on the Kurukshetra mud. It was a good formation—one that was flexible and would work well in offence or defence. In spite of our victory yesterday,

Dhristadyumna wasn't being too cheeky. There would be seven squares—four forward and three in reserve. Each square would be like a mini army, with chariots, infantry and a few elephants. It had been decided that Virata and Drupada would handle the reserve, while the young blood would go and splatter itself all over the field.

I walked towards the chariot park. Vishaka had been sent ahead with my armour and weapons. It was a warm morning. I hoped it wouldn't get hotter during the day.

I could make out young Abhimanyu from the back, standing next to Shikhandi outside the chariot park. He had been placed back in the reserves again today. This time, Arjuna had told Dhristadyumna to do so.

I went up to him, turned him around to face me and looked at him with all the reproachment I could muster.

He gave me his sweetest smile, 'Don't worry, Uncle. I'll be good today.'

My anger melted like the Gangotri glaciers in the summers. But I still shook my head disapprovingly, thinking of what to say. Abhimanyu saved my effort.

'I should get my chariot ready. Meet you in the field.'

He walked away jauntily into the park and Shikhandi spoke, 'I had a talk with him last night. I think I was able to make him understand what he can and can't do on a battlefield.'

I didn't say anything. I had never understood his fascination with killing. As if people's lives were acceptable collateral to get one's name written on a few pieces of parchment; their blood, the ink of his destiny. I shivered at the thought. A few days in the reserve would probably do him good. He needed to understand that killing people, even foot soldiers, should always be treated as an end in itself, and not the means to an end. As an act that needed to be performed because not doing it could actually be worse, not because it would get one glory.

I put on my armour and strapped up my helmet. My javelins were in their large leather sheaves and so were my stabbing spears. I carried a sword and an axe and a large shield as well as a small round one today. We left the chariot park and went towards the battlefield.

The Kauravas were waiting for us. They were arranged bizarrely. One flank made a crescent. Trigartas, by the look of it. And the other was a shield wall. I had never seen anything like this before. Satyaki was to my right. He would be the right person to ask.

'What's that called? It's half a crescent, and half a, well, square for all I can tell.'

'I haven't seen this one myself. Maybe Dhristadyumna has a better idea.'

We took our chariots to his square, which was positioned in the front and centre. He was with Arjuna, Bhima, Chekitana and Shikhandi when we approached.

'Can you tell the formation?'

'Half-crescent. Half-square. No name for it,' said Dhristadyumna distractedly. He was reluctant to have a conversation with me since yesterday. He could go to hell.

We took our positions in the forward squares and waited for the conches to sound. After his little rant yesterday, I had insisted on a forward position to much protest. I would show them all today.

A thin, bald man in white armour and dhoti stepped out in the neutral ground. He was unarmed and strode towards us purposefully, quite unafraid. This must be Susharma. The Trigartadesa king had made quite an impression yesterday.

He stopped a little distance from us and spoke loudly so that everyone up front could hear, 'Our vow is incomplete. Not for our strength of arms, but because of your cowardice. You ran yesterday, Arjuna. To kill a king who was old, weak, exhausted in battle and unable to fight. Is there glory in this? Honour? Today I challenge you to fight us. Only us. Not to run away until our dead line the ground or your blood bonds the soil. We await you on the right flank.'

I looked at Arjuna, whose face had turned white from anger. He gripped his bow so tightly, I feared it would crack. Krishna looked back at him from his charioteer's seat and drove the chariot to the right flank without saying a word. I heard Dhristadyumna tell Nakula, Sahadeva and Shikhandi to join him.

We stood in our positions. Arjuna took two squares of troops to deal with the Trigarta crescent. When they took their positions, the conches began to sound.

The day began.

I saw the Trigarta-lined crescent detach from the square and charge—white-coloured infantry, followed by white chariots. Our front ranks braced for the impact.

They joined combat with a loud, dull crunch. I looked ahead and said a prayer to the Lord for the well-being of my brother.

The Kaurava shield wall on our side stared impassively back at us. We waited for a few moments, hoping that they would attack. When this didn't happen, Dhristadyumna sounded an advance and we covered half the distance towards them when they started moving.

The shieldsmen wheeled to their flanks and ran to the back.

Behind them were foot soldiers and chariots in what appeared to be the shape of a circle.

I looked at Dhristadyumna, who looked unperturbed.

'Keep the advance going. Shields up. Spears out.'

Our front lines moved closer to the Kaurava circle. Could it even be called a line? It was like the round rim of a cup but with a gap in between.

Our men poured into the gap and within moments had been cut through with arrows. I could make out another circle within the first one, and maybe even one more.

Dhristadyumna called the infantry back. The Kaurava front rotated and a new set of soldiers took their positions while they marched towards us slowly. The gap in their front circle had widened now, almost daring us to enter.

'Chariots. Form a wedge and break through the ring.'

A chariot archer squadron formed and disappeared into the gap. I saw them circling around the second circle, caught in a criss-cross hedge of arrows. After a little while, I could see no more of them.

Dhristadyumna pulled the front line back as the Kaurava formation marched closer, crushing those who were unfortunate enough not to move in time. They took a few steps forward and rotated once more, circulating their troops.

I met Dhristadyumna and Bhima in the retreat.

Dhristadyumna started, 'Any ideas?'

Bhima shook his head. 'None. But we can't keep running forever.'

They looked at me and I shrugged, 'I don't know if it'll work. Maybe if we formed a shield wall and held our ground?'

We were contemplating this mode of action when

Abhimanyu ran into our midst.

Both me and Dhristadyumna were ready to kill him on the spot.

'It's a Chakravyuha. A many-tiered formation...rare... Concept formation... Hasn't been seen in a war ever!' he panted.

We waited for him to calm down and speak.

'It's called a Chakravyuha. Father had explained it to me once.'

It was pointless asking the boy how he escaped the reserves or how he had even been close enough to the front to see us get slaughtered.

'Did he tell you how to break it?' I asked.

'I can get in. But I'll need a little help getting out.'

'Explain.'

'It's like sewing. I'll be the needle, but I'll need a steady thread of troops behind me at all times, otherwise I'll get lost in the formation like the chariots that just went in.

'What do we have to do?'

'I'll lead a chariot wedge straight into the gap. Send men in behind me and we'll break it from the inside.'

'You? Why you?'

Abhimanyu looked at me as if I was an idiot, but since I was his uncle, he spoke softly, 'Because, I'm the only one who knows how to do it.'

'Tell me how it's done. I'll lead the force,' grunted Bhima.

'It's complicated, Uncle. We enter the gap in the first layer, then find the weakest point in the second layer, break through that and so on, till we reach the centre which is six layers from the outside.'

I heard Bhima mutter something uncomplimentary about

military theorists.

Abhimanyu continued, 'I'll create the path inside the vyuha for all of you to follow. Stick close behind me and keep feeding me troops. If any of the layers seal between us, I'll be trapped.'

I shook my head, 'It sounds too dangerous.'

Abhimanyu rolled his eyes, 'The Chakravyuha is coming closer, Uncle. It's the only way.'

He looked at Dhristadyumna and Bhima, who looked at me for direction.

It's always up to the eldest.

I nodded and grasped Abhimanyu by the shoulder as he was about to spring away.

'Okay, lad. You have your chance. But no tricks inside. Go safely and guide us in quickly. Once we're in, we'll join you.'

He smiled at me and scampered off to his chariot.

'No glory hunting!' I shouted to his back.

Dhristadyumna assembled a wedge of chariots for Abhimanyu almost instantly, each of which carried archers and infantry. He would be followed in by the Indraprastha contingent under Bhima, the Panchalas under Dhristadyumna and Yadavas under Satyaki. I would command the rest of the troops till they had secured a way in and join them later.

As an added measure, Bhima assigned Bali to be Abhimanyu's personal bodyguard in the vyuha.

I accompanied Abhimanyu as he joined his troops and reminded him repeatedly till his chariot took off that he was going in there to save the army, and not to become a hero.

ABHIMANYU

I sat with Pradyumna on a little cliff overlooking the sea of Dwaraka.

Father had come to Dwaraka after thirteen years and the city had welcomed his chariot with flowers and wine, dousing him liberally from their homes as he entered the city streets. Father smiled embarrassedly and looked down for the most part. He had entered the city and gone straight to Uncle Krishna's palace. I had been summoned from my lectures into the Hall of Conference where they sat. I entered the hall and sat in a corner. Father was speaking.

'I'm telling you, the Kauravas are not giving us a choice, Krishna. They aren't even letting us have Indraprastha. It's war.'

Krishna saw me and motioned me to come. 'We'll talk later. Recognize this young man, if you can.'

I hadn't seen him for thirteen years now. He had come to Dwaraka to ask for troops.

All talk of war was forgotten when he saw me, of course. And we spoke of more mundane things. Of my education, of my aunt and four uncles and, of course, his travels.

A trip to the south had taken him into the home of a military scholar. They had spoken till late in the night over glasses of Soma about formations, flanking manoeuvres, troop coordination and all the other little things that make war look complicated.

'His ideas were extraordinary for someone who has never set foot on the field. He showed me something he was working on—a formation shaped like a chariot wheel, a Chakravyuha.' He went on to explain the formation, and how it could be broken. Before he finished though, my mother entered the hall and monopolized the conversation.

So I went to meet Pradyumna and told him about the vyuha.

He didn't have much to say.

'Interesting.'

'Interesting? It's revolutionary.'

He didn't react. Our views on war were and will be entirely different for the next seven lives.

'The formation is all right. I am still at a loss to understand why anyone would think we needed another way of murdering people, much less conceive it.'

'Ha! Pacifist. You've always been one. Admit it.'

'I learn to fight so I can defend myself. Nothing more.'

I laughed.

'We learn to fight so people can fear us, Pradyumna. One day, their fear will turn to awe, and years later, it will become legend. War is nothing but a logical extension of our desire to be feared. That is the truth.'

He looked out into the murky grey waters. The sea wind drummed at our ears. And its sharp salty tang danced in our nostrils.

'You may be right, Abhimanyu. But consider this. I take fear to be a manifestation of love. When we fear for someone or something—it could be a person, wealth, power—it is because we cannot see ourselves complete without it. We then project our fear onto any person or object who is trying to threaten that which we love. This is called hate. War, or any invasion, is a manifestation of hate. When we hate something so much that we forget to protect what we fear for and seek to destroy what threatens it. I fight, therefore, to protect. And not to invade and destroy. That is why I will not enter the field of battle until someone threatens the ones I love.'

He was making his stance on Kurukshetra perfectly clear. He would not fight over kingdoms. It was a brave step considering almost everyone in the Yadavas had taken a side. For the past week, he had infuriated various factions who were requesting him to join them. The only person who was staunchly in his corner was Krishna.

'So what does Suyodhana fear...that makes him fight a war?'

My question made Pradyumna think. He looked into the ocean and allowed it to hypnotize him. His words came out softly, still raw from contemplation.

'I think he fears letting go of a kingdom he's spent thirteen years trying to build. To him, it is as much his child as you are to your father.'

I was about to change the topic when he asked me with a chuckle, 'And what do you fear, Abhimanyu? What makes you go to war?'

I had thought about it enough in my life since my father had left me on the shores of Dwaraka so many years ago. It was an easy answer. But I paused for gravity, nonetheless.

'Being forgotten.'

The conversation came back to me as I readied my line. I realized my hands were trembling when I strapped my helmet a notch tighter. I was giddy and my head felt heavy. Was I afraid? Of battle? I had been in too many of them. Was I afraid of entering the Chakravyuha? Perhaps. Did I need to be the one to break into it? Uncle Bhima had said he'd do it. There was still time. I could tell Uncle Dhristadyumna...

I closed my eyes and shook the thoughts out of my head.

Nerves. I hadn't felt them for a long time. I took a deep breath, said a prayer to calm myself and went to the head of the chariot wedge.

I took out my conch and blew a long peal. Sumitra looked behind at me and spoke, 'Putra, I don't have a good feeling about this.'

'That's what you always say, you old sissy.'

'No, putra. This time I'm serious. It's one thing to take on a single Kaurava in an open field, but we're going straight into their jaws. All of them will be waiting there. How many will you slay? You are yet young. Another should take your place.'

He looked at me with concern, and a tinge of hopefulness. Thinking that I would agree and step down from the chariot and go with my tail tucked between my legs to my uncles.

Not a chance, old man.

I ignored his plea. 'Prepare for the charge. I can see Guru Drona's standard back in the centre. That is where we will have to be by the end of the day.'

Our chariot wedge rumbled to life. I screamed my Yadava war cry of 'Dwaraka' as we hurtled towards the Chakravyuha.

Bali was beside me on his chariot. He raised his eyebrows and tilted his chin towards the gap, daring me to enter.

I couldn't possibly say no.

YUDHISHTHIRA

Abhimanyu's plan was working.

He and the men had managed to break into the vyuha. Behind him, Dhristadyumna and Bhima were getting ready to launch the Indraprastha Chariots.

Satyaki was with me as we watched the Kauravas desperately try to close the gap.

'Looks like fun. I wouldn't mind giving it a go.'

He looked at me and laughed.

Bhima had taken his squadron of chariots and headed towards the breach when a single chariot crossed into the gap that was beginning to swell with our men and started fighting them single-handedly.

It was the king of the Sindhus, Jayadratha. And he was soon joined by more chariots that ran over our troops and attempted to close the gap. A stream of axemen and macemen burst out from behind him and pressed our men hard in the flanks.

Bhima got off his chariot with his mace and advanced towards Jayadratha who also got down from his chariot with an axe and hacked down a soldier who tried to lance him. He ran at Bhima and butted him with his shoulder. Bhima fell down, slipping in the blood. Jayadratha heaved his axe and I held my breath but Bhima rolled out of the way just as it descended. More soldiers came to Jayadratha's aid and Bhima was soon outnumbered.

This was suicide. I told my charioteer to move in, when Dhristadyumna barred me with his hand and pointed at Chekitana who was running into the fray, evening the odds.

More Kauravas began filling the gap. And fewer of our

soldiers were making it out alive. Chekitana and his men had gotten to Bhima and pulled him away from the fight. Jayadratha had left the melee and had gone back into the gap, which was piling with the bodies of our dead and abandoned chariots.

The Kauravas set up a roar. The gap had finally closed... with Abhimanyu and his chariots in the vyuha's folds. I looked at Bhima who was gesturing Dhristadyumna to send more troops. Satyaki followed. And so did Ghatotkacha and his troubadours. I took a division of Panchalas and went in behind them.

Bhima, Satyaki and Chekitana combined their forces for an attack. Jayadratha sent foot soldiers to meet them with large platoons of archers behind.

Ghatotkacha's men went singing something I was too distraught to pay attention to. At close range, the bows just chopped them down and Dhristadyumna pulled them back before they got completely slaughtered. I saw Ghatotkacha hobbling back into our lines, an arrow in his knee.

I would go next.

ABHIMANYU

A Kaurava soldier with an axe raised his blade and jumped several feet in the air towards me. I didn't have time to aim, but at that distance I didn't have to. I pulled my string back and let the arrow fly. It smashed into his chest, stopping him mid-flight. He fell to the ground, coughed and lay back to die.

The Kauravas had closed in behind us, sealing the exit.

I turned around and saw the backs of their troops as they assembled frantically into position. We were trapped inside. There was no time to think. But I allowed myself the luxury anyway. Better to spend a few moments in contemplation, and arrive at the finish line a little late than never arrive at all, as Mother would say.

Two options presented themselves to me. The first, to pry open the gap that had just closed from the inside while my uncles worked their way in from the outside. And there was the second option to break further into the vyuha, causing as much destruction as we could, so that by the time the rest of our forces made their way in, they would have an easier path in front of them.

The first option had its flaws. There was no guarantee we would succeed. In attacking the first circle from the back, we would have exposed our own to the second layer and would be at their mercy.

The second option was more interesting. Slaughter our way into the centre. Maybe even kill a king or two. Uncle Bhima would crack the mouth open at some point, after all. But we would have to last out till he came, against more than three-fourths of their army.

Suicide.

An arrow whizzed by me, and stuck itself in the neck of an Indraprastha chariot archer. I looked in the direction it came from but the archer was gone.

In the distance I spotted Guru Drona's battle standard waving at me gently and made my decision.

Uncle Bhima didn't need my help getting in. It would be in everyone's interest if I created a path from the inside.

'Aim into the second circle. Fire at will.'

The bowmen in the chariots lifted their bows and the dull, rhythmic twangs of multiple bowstrings being released played out. A storm of arrows blew into the second layer and bodies fell like playing cards. We reloaded and fired again.

I saw Suyodhana's standard come fast towards the second line from the inside. He came up front, positioned his chariot in front of mine and took out his bow. This was too easy. In the time it took him to reach for his quiver I had shot him thrice in the chest. He fell down on his chariot floor and was taken away immediately.

Drona's son, Ashwatthama, came at me in a rage and fired twice. Both missed, and I pierced his arm with a crescent-headed arrow. He clutched it and swore at me. My next caught him in the thigh, and his charioteer wisely turned around and retreated.

The second circle wilted under our arrows and we triumphantly marched through to the third. I looked around for any familiar faces and wasn't disappointed. Kritavarma, Shakuni and Shalya were holding the circle. Before they could attack, I had fired an arrow that nicked Shalya in the neck and another that nearly took Shakuni's head off. Kritavarma fired in response, but I was able to catch the arc of his arrow and stepped aside. Bali on my left fired back and got him on the shoulder. Our advance force was doing well. The ferocity of our attack had surprised them.

Pradyumna used to tell me that on some days, and these days were very rare, a warrior could hold his destiny in the palm of his hand and direct it where he chose. Then every arrow, every sword strike or mace swing or axe chop would find its mark, compelled by his destiny. Those days were sacred, he told me. It had happened to him only twice; once during a siege and once while defending his village from a raid. And he had spent the night weeping in gratitude on both occasions.

'They weren't my hands holding the bow, Abhi. Someone, a force, was standing behind me…within me…showing me how to shoot. Taking the burden of killing all those people away from my hands.'

I looked at him curiously, almost doubting his sanity and he looked at me with pity. As if I would never understand till it happened to me.

It was happening to me now.

I was not drawing the bow or aiming the arrow. Or at least it didn't feel like I was. Did the rest of the advance force feel it too? The enemy was falling like flies.

I was so caught up in the carnage that I didn't notice the grey-bearded warrior, until he called out my name. It was Guru Drona. He had come up to bolster the line, by the looks of it. My knees almost buckled, and it took all the strength I had to lift my bow and acknowledge him. Guru Drona had come seeking to fight me!

I looked murderously at Bali and gestured that I would kill anyone in the Chakravyuha who came between me and Guruji.

Our chariots approached each other warily. I saw Bali, who had had the same ideas as me, hold the troops back. There were fewer of us now. Where was Uncle Bhima?

Guruji fired first, three arrows that made me duck into my chariot. I swore at myself for being so slow and got up and shot two back at him. He responded with two bolts that got me on the forearm and my shoulder plate. The old man could fight. I countered with a narrow, pointed arrow aimed at his face. It went a little higher and ripped through his helmet, causing him to fall back into his chariot.

Just as he fell, an arrow hit the side of my chariot. It was Radheya. He removed two more arrows and fired them one after another. One grazed my arm and the other scraped my breastplate. I replied with two arrows of my own.

The first arrow missed, but the second caught him square on his left shoulder. It must have been a good hit for he leaned down over to his charioteer and said something to him. The chariot turned and my third arrow hit its side. Radheya sat down, not giving me a clean shot, and his chariot scampered back into the layers of the vyuha. Drona and Radheya in one day!

YUDHISHTHIRA

I fell back into my chariot reeling. My head bounced hard against the wooden floor. Blood sprang into my mouth and sluiced down my nose. Jayadratha's arrows had hit me in the breastplate and helmet and knocked me down. I took a deep breath.

Our attack had failed. The gap was still closed. Bodies lay atop one another like bricks and we had to push aside our own dead to reach the enemy.

I had challenged Jayadratha. If we killed him, their spirit would die too. I had thrown an iron javelin, which cut down his chariot umbrella and had picked up another one when he shot me down.

I sat in my chariot fighting against the darkness that threatened to blanket me. This would not do. The boy was alone inside. I took another deep breath and somehow climbed back up to an upright position. My legs were weak and my eyes still a little bleary. The fall had hurt me worse than the arrows. I leaned against my chariot front and continued to suck long draughts of air. I ripped the helmet off my head and broke the arrow that had penetrated my breastplate. My stomach tensed and I felt the point of the arrow nestling into the skin. It was not a very deep wound. I would survive.

I looked back at Jayadratha and saw Bhima rush at him with a mace. Jayadratha leaped off the chariot just as Bhima slammed his mace into its side, cracking the vehicle. The horses reared in fright and the charioteer tried to run away, only to be picked off by a stray arrow.

Bhima bellowed and looked around for Jayadratha who had found another chariot. Bhima charged at him swinging his mace. This time, Jayadratha was ready with a bow. Three arrows found their mark. Bhima crashed to the ground and Jayadratha turned his attention to Chekitana who was leading a charge of his own.

A chariot came around Bhima's body, which was still moving. It was Satyaki. He dragged him into the chariot and brought him back to our lines. I looked back in front. Chekitana's attack had failed.

RADHEYA

The arrow had torn into my shoulder. I unclasped my armour at the top and pulled the crescent tip out slowly. When we were some distance away from the fight, my charioteer drew to a stop, stepped out and put turmeric and some antiseptic herbs on the wound and covered it with a clean bandage. We made our way back towards the centre.

The scene was grim as death. Drona, Shakuni, Kritavarma and Suyodhana were all in their chariots nursing their wounds. All apparently caused by the same boy.

Drona was talking about him like a teenager describing his first time.

'The boy is outstanding! He defeated all of us in one afternoon. Like Arjuna. Better than him at his age, I think. Who taught him, Kritavarma? What? Yes, I know the Yadavas, but who exactly?'

Dangerous talk when you're being whipped. Shakuni and Suyodhana were silent.

He went on some more, analyzing his duel with Abhimanyu to its gory details till Suyodhana had had enough.

'Guruji, I don't want to hear Abhimanyu's praises. I want to see him dead. How is it that the best bowmen in Bharatvarsha cannot bring down a boy? Stop singing his praises and go bring me his head.'

Suyodhana had crossed the line. Drona stared at him with those killing eyes and it was perhaps because of God's own protection that Suyodhana didn't melt or burst into a ball of flames or something equally terrible. They locked eyes for a few moments and Drona turned away in a huff.

Suyodhana had won a battle but not the one he wanted. His brother Sushasana came bounding up, enraged.

'Brother, let me have him. I'll tear his fucking guts out. Watch me.'

Suyodhana nodded and looked at me. He didn't need to say anything. I picked up my bow and followed Sushasana into the fourth circle where Abhimanyu had just arrived. The trouble with the Chakravyuha was that it got weaker as one approached the centre. Keeping the front lines intact was vital to its success. If he had enough chariots, Abhimanyu could even reach the centre and if the Pandavas broke through the front then...

There was no use thinking negatively. So I made a list of what was going well for us.

Number one. Jayadratha was taking care of business up ahead.

Number two. The boy's troops were getting tired.

I held my bow tightly praying that Jayadratha would hold fort.

Sushasana, meanwhile, had found Abhimanyu. It was a brief contest. As an archer, Sushasana was yojanas ahead of his elder brother, but still not good enough for a professional marksman. Two arrows pierced his left forearm and a third and fourth hit him in his right shoulder. Sushasana roared with futile rage and was silenced with an arrow that collided into his chest and threw him off his chariot, leaving his charioteer with the task of heaving him back into the lines.

I went in for my second round. A voice called out to me from behind.

'Guruji, let me try first.'

I looked back. Earlier in the day, I had made sure Laxman would be nowhere near the Samsaptakas for his bloody cheekiness. I had put him far back in the sixth layer of the Chakravyuha, far away from the front.

'Laxman, go back to the centre and join your father.'

He stood still in his chariot. His lower lip became a snarl. Even so, he turned his chariot around.

I approached Abhimanyu and this time the duel was even shorter. His first arrow broke my bow again and bloodied my left hand. This time, I didn't even need to tell my charioteer to turn and take cover. As I retreated, an arrow swooped by me towards Abhimanyu.

Laxman, you little prick.

He covered my retreat and went forward. An Indraprastha chariot blocked his path.

The warrior fired at Laxman, who stepped away smoothly from its path and replied with an arrow which the warrior ducked to avoid. Another arrow missed Laxman, who fired a terrific shot that hit the warrior's fingers, knocking a couple of them off. The bow fell from the warrior's grasp and he picked up a sword and a round shield and got off his chariot even as Laxman put an arrow through the neck of his charioteer.

The warrior ran at Laxman, effortlessly dodging his arrows as they stitched the earth around him. I watched Laxman closely, wondering what he was thinking and already planning how I would kill the warrior if he got too close to my boy.

It would have been easy for the lad to retreat. The warrior would never tail the chariot on foot. But Laxman wouldn't give up a kill so easily.

In the forests on the outskirts of Hastinapura, I had trapped a young panther and starved it for days before an archery test for my young shishya. I didn't want him shooting toy parrots off trees, like Drona's spoiled little charges.

They were made to face each other in a small arena. The panther, brought out of his cage, charged straight at the boy. Laxman panicked and fired four arrows that missed. Before the panther got too close, I put an arrow through its shoulder, which punctured its heart, killing it at the feet of the petrified child.

Later, I sat him down and told him how he should have approached the kill.

'Wait for your victim to kill itself. Don't die for your kill.'

He had smirked then at the clumsiness of the wordplay. But he seemed to have learnt the lesson.

He took his time and waited for his moment. The warrior was almost at the chariot horses when Laxman released his arrow. It stretched across the space between them and lodged in the warrior's thigh. He spun around and fell, giving Laxman enough time to draw another arrow. Laxman waited as the warrior raised his head unsteadily, and fired an arrow that crushed the warrior's nose and went out through the back of his head. The pain must have been terrible but the warrior didn't scream.

I was so proud of Laxman. He could take on Arjuna. He could take on a hundred like him.

ABHIMANYU

Bali died quickly. The arrow went through his skull and ended his time in the world without much fuss. His killer had shot well. But I was still going to avenge Bali. I called out to the warrior, who couldn't have been much older than me. His standard was yellow with a coiled viper in the rising sun. It turned gracefully towards me as our chariots faced each other.

He fired first. Two arrows back to back, almost parallel in their path. I tried to predict their line and twisted to my side. One of them grazed me on the left arm but it didn't go too deep. I turned, drawing an arrow of my own to fire.

An arrow slammed me in the chest and I landed heavily on the floor. The anxious face of Sumitra peered at me from above the chariot rim.

It was one of those days.

The arrow had penetrated my armour, but barely nicked my chest. I broke it off and rolled my eyes at Sumitra, who smiled.

I got up, arrow drawn and fired it straight at the enemy. He twisted to avoid my arrow. I followed his motion and as he drew another one, I aimed at the area between the base of his throat and his shoulders and fired.

The arrow went true, and before he could react, it had ripped into his throat. He coughed blood and made a horrible braying noise that didn't sound human. He tried removing the arrow, but it was barbed and stuck tight to his skin. He walked around his chariot and sank to his knees, gasping, almost choking in pain, searching for someone to help him.

For the first time in the day, I felt remorse. I took out an arrow and aimed carefully, even as my hands trembled slightly with guilt. The arrow with a sharp crescent head hit him a little above the barbed one and decapitated him. His body folded to the ground and I said a prayer for forgiveness.

You can't spend too much time thinking about the dead on a battlefield. Or waste your time fighting young, unknown warriors.

I turned around to look for Radheya.

RADHEYA

I watched as Laxman fell. It took all the strength I had not to surrender to my emotions and run out to help him.

I felt tired and stood in my chariot, not knowing what to do, hoping that circumstances would shake me into action. A chariot stopped to my left. It was Suyodhana. His face was pale. I didn't know what I could say to him. I might have started crying myself. I got off my chariot, walked to his, held him in my arms and put his head on my shoulder.

He pushed me and turned his face away.

Drona's chariot stopped next to ours.

'They are already in the sixth layer. We have to end this. Jayadratha will not last much longer.'

Suyodhana looked up, his face still pale, his arms shaking. He choked out something that none of us could understand.

He was in no condition to continue. I spoke to Drona,

'What do you suggest?'

'We gang up on him. You, me, Kritavarma, Ashwatthama and anyone else we can get. We surround him and use our bows.'

I was silent. It was a good idea. But it wasn't right—killing the boy as if it were a streetside brawl. Besides, killing anyone like that would not be considered honourable by the kings of Bharatvarsha. It was an unspoken rule that warriors of the nobility had to duel singly.

And this was no ordinary noble. This was the son of Arjuna. Humiliating him with a death that was better left for pigs in a hunt would have consequences. And there was Yudhishthira. Would he still accept me as his brother and put me on the throne after I had butchered his nephew?

My nephew.

Suyodhana pressed his eyes into his palms.

I made a decision.

'Tell Jayadratha to keep the line secure. Not even Yudhishthira can be allowed in.'

YUDHISHTHIRA

After Bhima fell, Dhristadyumna had attacked Jayadratha several times with no great success. The line still held firm. I could make out some commotion inside the vyuha. The men were still fighting. Maybe Abhimanyu was alive.

We had become mechanical in our movements. Make an

attack, get beaten, pick ourselves up and repeat. I had failed in four attacks already. In the most recent one, a blunt javelin had hit me in the chest, throwing me face-first into the mud.

The mud tasted different. I wiped it off my eyes and saw the ground. A black layer of blood was spread over it, obscuring its identity completely.

I had sent the boy in, and now he was trapped because I couldn't get past a king who wasn't even a Maharathi. I would not be able to face Arjuna if something happened to his son. What would I tell him? I had to bring back Abhimanyu or none of us could return. Bhima had been badly wounded for his efforts. I could not do less.

I got back on the chariot and made straight for Jayadratha again. I lifted an iron-tipped javelin and took careful aim at his chest. He saw me coming and drew an arrow just as I released my weapon. It flew clean through the air and descended towards his chest. He lifted his bow to protect himself, jumping off the chariot at the same time. The javelin smashed his bow but missed him.

I lifted another javelin. A bronze this time, no irons were left, and aimed for Jayadratha. He was already on his chariot with another bow drawn.

He fired. I threw.

I didn't see if my javelin hit, but his arrow took me on the chest. I fell off the chariot for the third time that day into the dark mud.

RADHEYA

We didn't say a word as we approached Abhimanyu. Drona would take him from the front, with Kritavarma and a Gandhara prince. I would attack him from behind, with Ashwatthama and an Atirathi called Brihatbala.

He had reached the centre, that boy, with enough chariots to still pose a threat. So much for the Chakravyuha's promised invincibility.

Drona called him out, luring him away from the protective cordon of chariots that surrounded him and Abhimanyu took his chariot towards him, intent on a duel. This was our cue. We surrounded him.

He did not suspect us even for an instant.

He drew an arrow and placed it on his string. Behind him, I had already drawn my bow and before the boy could shoot, my arrow picked off his bow. I cursed. The arrow was meant to hit him on the shoulder. He looked back in genuine surprise and probably thought it was a mistake on my part.

My next arrow rid his mind of doubt. It got him in the left shoulder even as arrows from Ashwatthama and Brihatbala pierced him on either side. Meanwhile, Drona had killed his charioteer, and Kripa and Kritavarma had shot his horses.

Everyone drew their bows back and fired for a second time.

The boy really was invincible. He just stood on his chariot. There were arrows all over his breastplate. One was lodged in his helmet and another was even stuck in his thigh. Six arrows. They should have killed him, or at least knocked him down.

We watched as he bent into his chariot and took out a sword and round shield. I ordered four spearmen to go and finish the job so that we wouldn't have to. All the same, everyone still stood with arrows drawn. The spearmen circled the boy as he cut the shafts of the arrows protruding from his chest with his sword. They attacked him.

One by one, the idiots.

I shouted at them to kill him together. Together! But that only confused them. In an instant, the boy had run his sword through one of them and smashed his shield into another's face while the other two stood gaping. He turned to face them now. They stepped back hesitatingly. I couldn't make out who outnumbered who. I screamed at them again, which jolted them into action. They charged at him together, but he stepped aside and cut one's neck with a backstroke. The remaining soldier stood paralysed with fear, and the boy walked over to him calmly and slid his sword into his gullet.

This could not go on much longer. And for once, Drona and I had the same idea. My arrow hit the boy's left hand that held the round shield, while Drona's hit the right, severing two fingers. The sword slipped from his hand and he clutched the bleeding stumps of his finger but did not cry in pain, instead he sucked in air sharply, like a child who's stubbed his toe.

Brihatbala and Ashwatthama's arrows missed him while Kritavarma hit him twice in the back. He turned to face them. I drew again and got him in the back. He fell forward, near a broken chariot.

He lay there for a little while and we looked at each other, wondering whether it was safe to go and check if he was dead. I looked around for infantry to do the dirty work when Brihatbala swore. The boy was getting up. Five arrows flew at him at the same time. One found his shoulder. He didn't even notice it as he leaned on the chariot, slowly trying to get up.

When death is close, dignity abandons you first, along with its toadies—restraint and poise. I've seen men use their nails and teeth to protect their hides.

What I saw that day was different.

The boy held on to his dignity, even as it probably howled to get out. He was composed and in full control of his senses. I could not bring myself to fire at him again. I looked at the others one by one. Their faces wore guilt.

He stood on shaky legs and nearly fell down against the chariot. I heard a cry from behind and looked. His troops were rallying and attempting a rescue. Ashwatthama and Brihatbala used it as an excuse to disengage, even though there were enough soldiers around us to keep the boy's forces out.

I looked back and saw the boy with his hands around a chariot wheel lying on the ground. The wheel must have weighed more than a grown human being. And I watched as he got on his knees and hefted it onto his shoulders. He raised it high above his shoulders and walked towards me, his legs trembling with the effort.

For a moment, I didn't know whether to kill him, or let him kill me.

He raised the chariot wheel higher and broke into a jog, then into a run. I fired two arrows at the wheel which tipped him over.

He crawled slowly, trying to get on his feet.

A boy walked past Drona's chariot into our little circle of death and shame. It looked like Sushasana's son, a boy not much older than Abhimanyu or Laxman, called Surmashana. He had a mace in his hand and walked quickly but silently behind

Abhimanyu, who was on one knee. He lifted the mace, slowly, not attracting his attention.

Abhimanyu raised his head and looked at me. Surmashana swung the mace down, like an executioner, to the back of his head. Abhimanyu's eyes rolled and he fell into the dust. Surmashana took a step back and lifted the mace again and brought it down on the fallen boy's head again.

I thought of telling Surmashana to stop, but then remembered Laxman.

Surmashana continued smashing Abhimanyu's skull till his body lay behind a red-grey mass of pulp.

Finally, a man ran in and snatched the mace from Surmashana.

It was Yuyutsu. He pushed Surmashana away and walked towards me shaking with anger.

'Six men against one boy. Did you think this was fair?'

I didn't answer him.

'Did you ask him to surrender?'

'He wouldn't have.'

'Did you ask him?'

'No.'

'The whole of Bharatvarsha will hear of this. Tomorrow, the bards will sing of our shame. We can't even kill a boy with honour.'

'He's dead. That's all that matters.'

'He's dead, Radheya. At what cost? There can be no peace with the Pandavas now. No hope of conciliation. We're doomed to kill our cousins, or die in the attempt. But they're not your family, are they? Of course, you don't care!'

He walked away, flinging the mace to the ground.

I called out to his back as he walked away.

'I care about Suyodhana. What about you?'

THE THIRTEENTH NIGHT

YUDHISHTHIRA

My head was paining when I woke up. I was in the back of a chariot that wasn't mine. The charioteer provided answers, 'Lord Satyaki, sire. He found you and told me to take you back.'

'Is...is the battle over?'

'A little while back, sire. Yes'.

'What happened?'

He was silent. I spoke gently.

'Tell me what happened, charioteer.'

'We weren't...I think...I believe they... sorry, sire...'

Numbness has a way of protecting you. An invisible coat of paint that washes over and covers any chink or crack of emotion that may otherwise show on your face. I listened dully to his desperate attempts to soften the blow. Then I remembered.

'The boy. What happened to Abhimanyu? Did we break the vyuha?'

Silence, again.

'Speak man, or I'll rip your tongue out.'

His voice trembled, 'He's...he's no more, sire. I'm sorry.'

The numbness prevented me from breaking down in front of the unknown charioteer. I felt a wave of tiredness hit me. I wanted to sleep desperately, but I had to know what happened.

'Tell me everything you know, charioteer.'

By the time we reached the camp, I had learned all about

the way the Kauravas had murdered my nephew. My body lifted itself off the chariot and walked to the council tent, drawn like a heavy plough by my leaden senses. If Arjuna wasn't there, he would be in his tent. If he wasn't in his tent, I would scour the battlefield. I would enter hell, but I would speak to him.

I was the eldest. What would I tell him? What could I. My mind flitted across the familiar constructs and phrases we use in lieu of emotion to convey our regret of a person's bereavement. 'I am sorry for your loss.' 'He was brave till the end.' 'He's in a happier place now.' I couldn't possibly tell him any of this.

An old sage I had met once had spoken to me on the nature of death. At the time, I remember being inspired by his conversation, by the resolute ambivalence of it, by the fact that he had no clear answers, and yet had clarity.

He had spoken in contradictions. He told me then that living in fear of death was to fear living itself. That life and death were bound to each other and yet separate from another. People went about their daily lives denying death's existence, and yet it was all around them all the time. He had told me that grief should not be felt for those who had died, but for those who were living. After all, wasn't death absolute and life unpredictable? I had asked him whether he believed that death was a passageway to another world. And he replied that perhaps life itself was the passageway.

To feel the momentary light of wisdom, and to live in its glow every day are two entirely different things. No matter how much you try, there are some things you can't internalize.

I entered the tent, praying that the Lord would show me

a way. It was quiet but not empty. They had gathered with the same intent—Virata, Drupada, Chekitana, Nakula, Shikhandi, Sahadeva, Dhristadyumna and Bhima.

Arjuna walked into the tent followed by Krishna. I could see from his face that he had already heard.

No one said anything.

I went to him, my eyes shining with tears. I pressed him against my chest and felt his frame tremble against mine.

I held him close. As I hadn't since we were boys.

Bhima walked me to my tent long after the camp torches had stopped burning. We were silent till we reached my tent. He spoke, his voice heavy with sadness.

'It's my fault. I promised the child I would come. I...I tried...'

'It's not your fault, Bhima. If anyone is to blame, it is me. I sent a boy with ten days on the field to fight warriors with several years behind them.'

He sniffed, 'They still weren't able to kill him cleanly, the bastards.'

I nodded. He looked at me listlessly, wiped his moustache with the back of his hand and walked away, a lumbering ghoul, into the darkness.

A thought breached the dullness in my head. And the clarity I received with it shamed me, even as it gave me pride. In a way, Abhimanyu's death was symbolic. The Chakravyuha was an elaborate metaphor for human life. Its layers represented our fears and insecurities. The chariot represented us. And the centre represented what we wanted to become. We had to move the chariot through every layer, destroying our fears one by one till we reached the centre.

It was important to enter the Chakravyuha, and reach its

centre, and then exit it as gracefully as possible.

I lay on my bed and the day defeated me for the last time.

RADHEYA

After the boy fell, we butchered the men with him and formed our layers once again with whatever troops we had left. Jayadratha had been magnificent. Not one Pandava soldier had gotten in after the initial rout. He managed to keep them out even after Abhimanyu had been killed, right up to the very end, when the Pandavas turned and marched away shamefaced.

I believe our soldiers didn't let him set his feet on the ground that entire night.

The camp was a carnival in the evening. Sura was flowing freely. Spits of meat roasted outside in large, happy fireplaces. And double rations were given to all, again. Song and dance were allowed for a brief while, till the lights went out. After two days of suffering defeat in the battlefield, the soldiers finally had something to celebrate. I had gone back straight to my tent for a bath, hoping to avoid any celebrating soldiers. My heart was not in it.

So. I would never be king...not in this birth, at least.

If I wasn't killed on the battlefield, I would, at best, be Suyodhana's second-in-command as he made his own legacy for the Kurus. No robes of royalty. No throne. No gem-encrusted crown. No noblemen hanging around for my commands. I was casually calculating my losses when I heard some commotion outside my tent. A few soldiers had wandered outside the area of leisure. A voice silenced them, as much as it was humanly possible to silence a horde of drunken soldiers, and a head stuck into my quarters.

'Beg your pardon, Lord. The soldiers are humbly requesting the pleasure of an audience with yourself.'

It was Shatrujeet. The man was drunk or trying hard to get there.

I stepped out to see countless red, happy faces around me, beaming with pleasure. I took a step back and collided into someone standing between me and my tent opening. Before I could say anything, they had lifted me on their shoulder. Shatrujeet was shouting, spraying everyone generously with his spit.

'Lord Radheya. It was all his idea...his formation...the Chak... Chaka. Chakavyuha!'

The soldiers roared, and I didn't bother telling him it wasn't my formation.

'Lord Radheya! Long Live Lord Radheya!' I could hear them scream even after they had set me down after a whole round of the camp.

Before he left, Shatrujeet took me to the side and whispered gleefully, 'Three gold chests, sire. For your head.'

I walked to the council tent and saw that the celebratory mood had spilled over here as well. Drona was smiling as he spoke to his son. He saw me and walked up to me and gave me a hug. All thoughts of Abhimanyu were behind us now, though I suspected they would haunt us later. Sushasana was telling everyone, 'Surmashana, my son, he killed Abhimanyu. He killed him.'

Jayadratha was the prime attraction of the tent. Everyone wanted to know how he had kept back all the Pandavas, and more importantly, where had he been the past twelve days? The smile was stiff, as were his movements, but I could tell he was enjoying the attention.

Only two people in the tent were not sharing in the revelry. One of them was Yuyutsu. He sat in a corner, brooding, and glared at me as I walked past.

'You've doomed us, Radheya. All of us. You and Guruji. How could you all be so stupid?'

I left him even as he spewed more hatred at my back. Some of the other kings looked sympathetically at me. I had heard the allies were openly calling him a traitor now, after his outburst on the field.

He was right. We had gone down a road that would end with the death of all the soldiers parked on at least one side of the field. There would be no turning back. I had doomed us all. And yet, my conscience felt clearer then it had for the past three days.

The other man in the tent who wasn't sharing in the joy was forced to speak to everyone. When they heard about Laxman's death, the allies took it upon themselves to offer their condolences. He listened to them all, even though it must have taken all his strength to stop himself from storming out of the room.

I spoke to him when they finally left him alone.

'Suyodhana, get some rest. Tomorrow will be another long day.'

He nodded, expressionless.

I continued, not sure of what I was saying, 'Laxman fought

better than all of us today.'

I would like to think that the thought comforted him even if my words didn't. He stared at the floor and said softly, 'I'll kill them all, I promise. They won't live to see Indraprastha. None of the brothers will ever be king.'

I just nodded and put my arm around him.

Epilogue

The old warrior lay in the tent.

He heard the sound of shuffling and his tent opened briefly. This time, he didn't even make an effort to see who had come. What use was it now? Death would, in fact, be a mercy, given the pain he was in.

'It's me, Grandsire.'

Radheya.

'So you've come back...without a crown on your head, without your brothers, without anything. Just the way we met last time.'

Radheya stood silent looking at the ground.

'How did it feel, putra? Did you feel safe in the shade of six warriors? I heard it took a seventh to land the final blow. Was it because you were too scared to do it yourself?'

The effort made him cough. Radheya picked up the jug of water lying on the table beside the bed and poured him a tumbler.

'Easy, Grandsire.'

'Even if you go to them on your knees and beg forgiveness, they won't accept you. Who...whose idea was it to kill the boy in such an idiotic way?'

'It was Drona.'

'I should have never made him Guru. He should have remained a training instructor to the end of his days. But you, Radheya, you had an entire kingdom at stake.'

'I'm not sorry for killing him.'

His bluntness silenced Bhishma.

'As to why I did it, Suyodhana trusts me. He trusted me with a kingdom when I was a charioteer. He trusted me with protecting the Kuru empire when he didn't know I was a Kuru. And he trusted me with the life of his son. I betrayed him once today by letting Laxman die. I don't think I'll be able to do it again.'

'If you became king, you could have saved his life.'

'There is still time for that.'

'Stupid boy. You will always be his puppet. Never anything more, don't you see?'

Radheya shrugged, 'If that's what you think...'

Bhishma sighed and was silent for a long time before he spoke.

'I've watched over the Kuru Empire for more than fifty summers. I have raised three generations of its princes. I did everything I could to stop you boys from killing each other, even sent the Pandavas away for thirteen years. After all this, I must see my life's work go to dust.You were my last hope, putra. I had hoped that you would sacrifice your loyalty to Suyodhana for the good of the Kurus.'

Radheya went forward and touched his feet. Bhishma raised his right hand weakly in blessing.

'But who should have been sacrificed? Suyodhana or the

Kurus? I fear you'll find out very soon.'

Radheya walked away. As he left the tent, he heard Bhishma's voice call out to him.

'I pray for you boy, all of you.'

Radheya walked out of the tent enclosure and climbed on the horse that was waiting outside. He rode back to the Kaurava camp.

It was a starless night in Kurukshetra. But the moon was bright and lit his path. A solitary tree standing on the road shivered with ecstasy, its leaves sighing with pleasure as the wind caressed it with its long, gentle fingers. A wandering minstrel sat under the tree, a small fire keeping him company. He had a one-string instrument in his hand and a voice that carried down through the lonely road.

'A hundred thousand men he slayed
their bodies shining with blood.
Nine hundred elephants, eight thousand chariots lay
ornaments embellishing the mud.
Two thousand princes he slew
with his bow, his axe and his mace.
Till the treachery of six
brought shame to the Kuru race.
A hundred thousand men he slayed...'